I'm Not a Little Girl (Really!)

A Lesbian Spanking & Ageplay Novel

Volume 6

By Alex 'Lexy' Bridges

Warning: This story contains adult content, including ABDL, spanking, lezdom, ageplay, and other fetish themes, and is intended for adults 18 years and older only. All character are adults 18 years of age or older.

Acknowledgements

Thank you to all the readers who encouraged me in my writing, all my Patreon supporters, and all the Daffys and Marys of the world.

About the author

Alex, who also goes by Lexy, is a life-long ABDL and kink enthusiast turned author focusing on ABDL, spanking, erotic humiliation, lezdom, femdom, feminization, and ageplay. Alex's stories focus on believable characters, deep relationships, and kinky fun times between loving and loveable protagonists.

You can find more stories from Lexy at allmylinks.com/alexbridges.

Forward

This is Volume 6 in a series about the adventures of Mary and Daphne, the cutest and kinkiest lifestyle domestic discipline ageplay couple you'll find this side of fantasy land.

This volume picks up right where Volume 5 leaves off. To learn how our newlyweds got where they are now, check out:

Volume 1
https://www.amazon.com/dp/B08Y84SH6Z

Volume 2
https://www.amazon.com/dp/B08ZNQXWDM

Volume 3
https://www.amazon.com/gp/product/B091HRQ94L

Volume 4
https://www.amazon.com/dp/B093T73HY7

Volume 5
https://www.amazon.com/gp/product/B096QW6GRT

And if the backstory isn't of interest (though it's very interesting – promise!), dive on in!

Table of Contents

Chapter 1: It's Not What It Looks Like

Mary sickens me. The way she had two weeks off work and then was excited to go back? It's just not right! No one should be so positive and healthy minded. It's like she's got a long–release Focusyn capsule placed under her skin back before they took that stuff off the market.

I, by contrast, possess the much healthier approach to the end of vacations and was bummed enough for both of us. I had a new appreciation for our childhood golden retriever (Goldie, because we're a creative bunch) and how he must've felt when we went back to school after Christmas. And Mary was only downstairs, but she closed the door so she could catch up on emails. I say just delete the emails and if it's important they'll email you again.

Meanwhile, I was working on my New Year's resolution to live in a more organized house. At least, that's my story, but really, I was just bored and decided to inventory our toys. Some of the stuff in there sometimes scares the crappin' crud outta me out of context. I need context or my reaction is more like, "It's gonna go where!?!?" All the magazines call it foreplay, but me, I call it context.

And so many impulse purchases! That's the real reason they keep this stuff in the back of the stores; if they kept it by the register with the other impulse products, we'd be going home with chocolate bars and cheese popcorn and great big … Anyhoo, um, did I mention I had a dog named Goldie growing up? I'm wholesome like that.

And as I was straightening and organizing, I found so many ways to sort the toys, too. By size. By color. By things that sting and things that slap and things that leave welts and things that leave bruises. By things that make a noise and things that make you make a noise and things that do both. By things for when I'm bent over chairs and things for when I'm bent over Mary and things for when I'm legs up and flat on my back. I was just arranging and rearranging and playing a weird game of horizontal Tetris and made piles of things we use and things we sometimes use and things we thought we'd use and don't, and a large pile of things (that despite its immense size contained just three items) that I dubbed "the aspiration pile" because clearly we were kidding ourselves thinking either of us could … Anyhoo …

Now, before we go any deeper down this rabbit hole (hehe!) I should tell my side of the story, also known as the truth. I've never misled you, for it is not in my heart to be untrue. It's just that, like Goldie would sometimes act out when we went back to school, I was bored. What started as a made-up chore and trip down memory lane (which runs right through the heart of the red-light district), got me to thinking about what a shame it is we have things we bought and rarely use. I'm very environmentally conscious, so just like Mary said way back when if she was going to make me wear pullups it was only right that she also make me use them (some illogical logic that woman has), I thought it would be wrong to not give some of the things we never use a second chance. And I'll also say I got a second chance or two in my time, and I'm a big believer in them. It was an act of idealism I committed.

Or tried to commit with one such toy (let's call it an action figure with karate chop motion and poseable doodads) when I decided there was a reason we didn't like it and made a new pile I called the "just throw it out pile." Before I could sample one of the other items from the Island of Misfit Toys, my phone dinged, and then something happened on Facebook, and then something else happened on Facebook, and then I decided to finally learn what TikTok is, and then someone was wrong on the internet and had to be corrected, which is when I heard this voice from the doorway say, "O. My. God."

"Hi Mary. How's work going?" Not well, judging by the look on her face. A rictus of horrified amazement, one might call it. Don't see what could've happened in just the last two hours to make her …

"Omygod! Not what it looks like! I was, um …"

"You're not wearing any pants."

"O, those, yeah …"

"And you're surrounded by piles of sex toys."

"I wouldn't call them piles. More like, um … stacks. Bet you didn't realize how many things we never use."

"Not anymore!"

"But heh muh fuh ing just one!"

"Your face is as red as that pile." O, yeah, the red pile. "What on earth are you doing up here?"

"Straightening up."

"Daffy, if this is how you straighten up, you won't ever walk straight again."

"Buhahaha! I mean, that's inappropriate." She has such a potty mouth sometimes. That joke was a little on the nose. If it were me, I'd have gone with something like 'if that's how you straighten up, I woulda begged to go to

Bible camp,' but blasphemy gets dealt with harshly in our house.

"Uh–huh. Sorry," Mary said, "I know how embarrassed you can be on the subject of sex."

Did she just ... "Don't you roll your eyes at me." Eye rolling is my thing. She can't have my thing. And then she picked up one of the things.

"I forgot we had some of this stuff. Which one of us bought this one?"

"I don't remember."

"Well, someone's eyes were too big for someone's wife." Well, my eyes were like saucers watching her pick that up and wave it about all threatening and sexy like. "You're not gonna faint, are you? You and your delicate sensibilities."

I swallowed. My tongue stuck in my throat. I needed some water or something to lubricate ... Anyhoo ... "Um, that's the aspiration pile."

"Ha! I'll say! What an awful mess you've made."

"Things often get messy before they get clean again."

"Didn't Martha Stewart say that when she was broadcasting from prison?"

"Maybe I should clean up after myself."

"That reminds me." O, I just bet it did. When things remind her, she soon reminds me of them. "Did you ever wear that French maid outfit I bought you back at the start of quarantine."

"A couple of times, and you took my feather duster and ... Mhmm, I did."

"If you're in a cleaning mood, why don't you put that on and do some cleaning?"

"We cleaned yesterday." Another thing that's more evidence of Mary being too healthy minded. Who cleans the day after they get back from vacation? Like anyone was home to make a mess?

"But we didn't clean our toys. I think you should put that outfit on and clean each one of these by hand in the sink."

"This feels like a punishment." I mean, we bought dishwasher–safe toys for a reason.

"Funny you say that."

"Of course it is," I said with no mirth. Mirthless.

"You're going to clean every toy we own by the time I'm done with work, and then I want you to choose three toys for me to inspect, and if they're not each immaculate, I'll have no choice but to use them on you."

"O. Hehe mmmmm ooo." See how classy and sexy and not at all like a doofus I can be at sexy time? "Any three I want?"

"How about one toy that smacks naughty bottoms, one toy that gets worn, and one inside toy."

Inside toys? These were not traditionally the type of toys one uses out of doors. "But they're all inside …" *Ooo, now I see what she's getting at.*

"Blushing again. I'll give you something to blush about."

"(Gulp)."

Chapter 2: I Didn't Mean to Be a Bitch

"Am not."

"That kind of answer says otherwise," Mary said about my answer. Reviewing my answer like she's queen of the damn answers.

"Urgh!" SWAT!

"Park yourself in the corner," SWAT, "and no stomping."

"I'll stomp if I want to," I said not as under my breath as I thought.

"Little girl, you are testing all my patience today."

So what am I not? Dripping with attitude. I don't know what that dripping sound is. I don't even hear anything. I'm not having a serious case of the back talk. You are! This whole court room is talking back and stuff! Nyah!

But because I am reasonable, I am open to the possibility that Mary has a point. But if she does, it's only because she's right, and no one likes people who are right all the time.

"Front and center," Mary said. I turned around and walked over to her trying to see what implement she'd chosen. A freshly cleaned implement, I'll add. I stood in front of her, and she took my pants down, "Little girls get spanked on their bare bottoms, don't they, Daphne Ann," she said as she tugged me into position over her knee.

"I'm not a little girl," I said as I settled in.

"You're pouting around like one, and I know just the way to adjust that attitude."

Well, there I was, over Mary's knee getting spanked again. Sometimes I wish I could fast forward through it, not because it hurts and not because I don't like it and not because I don't not like it but because I've been there, I've done that, and we have photos to prove it. Really.

"Are you listening to me," Mary asked.

"Yes, geez!"

"Then what'd I just say?"

"To … not do it again?" SMACK! *Dammit!*

"I said, little lady, that you need to fix your attitude and stop taking out your bad mood on me (SMACK). No more sass (SMACK). No more moping (SMACK). No more rolling your eyes (SMACK) like you just did (SMACK)."

"You can't even see my eyes!"

"Did you just roll them?"

"(Sound of a tumble weed blowing through town)."

"Uh–huh (SMACK!)." I won't spell out the other spanks, but there were more than a few, bordering on a lot.

"Ow! I'm sorry! Ow ow OW! Marrrry … Urgh! Eeeep! … O eh eh! (Sniffle). I'm sorry. I OWW! Eheh eheh eheh waaaaaaah!"

Okay, sue me; I'll spell out some more – SMACK SMACK SMACK! "Am I making myself clear?"

"(Repentant wookie noise)."

SMACK! "Am I going to need to spank for this issue again this week?"

"(Injured moose sounds)."

SMACK! "Good. Sit up for me."

"(Squeaky toy noises) And I'm (foghorn). (Sniffle)."

"You're okay. C'mon and sit up for me," Mary cooed at me. "Up you go."

"(Meeping noises)."

"Of course you can," she said and gave me permission to bury my face in her chest.

I'm having a rough year, and it's only the third day. 2021 is ~~too damn much~~ exactly like 2020, and the return from our vacation was like a return to the dumpster fire of boredom, crappy news, and anxiety. Not like I meant to take it out on Mary, but since she's the only person around, who else am I gonna take it out on except nobody because no one did anything to me. I just got snippy while we were doing the dishes.

To my credit I didn't say anything I shouldn't have. I just gave off this vibe that said it all for me, specifically something like 'The way you're loading the dishwasher angers me beyond a point which is reasonable.' Why the heck do people fight over the dishwasher anyway? It was just … I was in one of those moods where if I'd seen a rock, I'd have been mad at the rock. Mary, being Mary, didn't even give me any attitude back. Just a couple warning glances that I saw, understood, and ignored, and then off to the corner to get to the bottom of me.

"Look up for me," Mary said. "O, your poor eyes are so red. C'mon, let's go wash your face." I got up off her lap. "Step out," she said and got my leggings off from around my ankles.

"(Sniff)," I sniffed on the way to the bathroom.

"Hop up," Mary said, and I sat down on the vanity.

"Ow."

"Butt hurt?"

"Mmm."

"Wasn't the fun kind of spanking, was it?"

"No."

"Or the not–fun kind that gets fun at the end," she remarked as she wet a washcloth.

"No. I'm sorry."

"Hold still for me, baby," she said and wiped the tear streaks off my face. "Honk."

I blew my nose and forgot to remind her I'm not a duckling. "Because 2021 is just like 2020," I said.

"What?"

"Why I was in a bad mood."

"But you're not in a bad mood now?"

"I hope not," I said with that I–might–start–crying–again sound in my voice.

"Let's get you ready for bed."

"It's only 7:30."

"Are you going to tell me you're not tired?" Taking my hand and leading me to bed like she's gentle and wonderful and nice to me and stuff.

"I'm sorry," I said again.

"And I forgive you. Lay down?"

"Do I gotta," I asked as she went to my dresser and got a diaper out. I wish she'd stop putting those there. And where the heck did the rest of my panties go? I know I used to have more pairs, including a lot more pairs that didn't come from junior miss departments at our regions fine and not-so-fine apparel retailers.

"Yes, you do … Do you want one of the other ones?"

"Those are for when I've been good," I reminded her of the terms we negotiated for the cloth diapers.

"They're for whenever I say." She put the one back and went into the closet and came back out with one of those other ones. It's not that I want to wear one at all, but since I don't have a choice, I like those ones better. They feel nicer. They're snugger, and I like that. Not nearly as nice as Mary hugging me down there though.

"I don't like 2021," I said.

"I think," Mary said, "we shouldn't even talk about 2021 until we've been vaccinated. Lift."

"We're gonna lose a whole nother year." Mary tugged at my hips and sealed the velcro tight.

"Look at me. We're not losing anything. We have each other, and if the whole world burns down around us, having each other makes us the luckiest people ever. Do you believe that."

"Of course I do. It's just … " I sighed. "I don't like pandemic me. She's moody and mean."

"I like pandemic you as much as I liked pre–pandemic you. More even, and do you know why?"

"Because you love me?" She has to say stuff like that because she loves me.

"Because it's reminded me of how strong you are, and how proud I am of you."

"(Sniff)."

She sighed and went to my nightstand. "Here," she said and took out a Xanax. "And no telling me you don't need it tonight."

I took the pill and swallowed it dry. "I'm not so strong."

"Scoot over." I did and she laid down next to me. "You have more reason than most people to be scared during all this, and quitting your job right before was also

17

scary, and you've been stuck here and more isolated than anyone else we know. I think you need to give yourself credit for all of that."

I'm not especially good at giving myself credit, which probably sounds odd to you since I've told you just how much I'm an example for the world's youth and your rightful queen second only to Mary and you should be sending me gifts of peanut butter and precious gem. All of which is true, but that's different. I didn't respond to Mary and instead said, "I don't mean to take stuff out on you."

"I know. I don't like it either, and I hope the red bottom I just diapered will remember to deal with those moods in better ways."

"Bad moods and PMS are no excuse for being a bitch," I quoted the rule from very early on in our relationship. Bad moods caused by a pandemic are no exception.

"That's right, and you got a spanking to snap you out of it."

"Mhmm. Thanks for that. Sorry I was a bitch about that, too." Sometimes I forget getting my butt spanked is for my own good, literally. I suppose I got taught a lesson, and my butt would hurt enough to remind me, and maybe if I hadn't been such a sourpuss I would've realized I just needed a paddle bounced off my butt to put my sorts back in order.

"Do you feel a little better now at least?"

"Mhmm. I was just angry."

"At what?"

I shrugged. "Like I said, 2021. I … It was good we went on vacation, but coming back and then you going back to work and 2021 just being like 2020, it was just, like, 'o yeah, pandemic reality.'"

"I know."

"But you don't take it out on anyone."

"I just took it out on your butt … and I totally lost my cool with tech support this morning, so there's that."

"Heh."

"But we should find better ways to deal with it. That's your project for tomorrow: coming up with one short–term, one medium–term, and one long–term thing to put your energy toward. We'll talk about it after work."

"Kay. Can I make a rule, too?"

"Go for it."

"You have to stop work at noon every day and have lunch with me, no matter what. I'll make us something."

"I promise, Daffy. I'll put it on my calendar every day. Which panties do you want?"

"Can't I just wear these without them?" Wasn't that enough?

"Only I'm allowed to take this off, and if you potty in them they won't stop it from getting on the sheets. And it's only 7:45."

"… The white ones." Back into the closet she went and came back out.

"Gimme a footsie."

"You don't have to babytalk at me," I reminded her.

"You don't have to always pretend you hate this every step of the way."

"But I do, is the thing."

"Always have to pretend, or hate it?"

"(Wind whistling through trees two counties over)."

"Lift … there. All tucked in. Take your shirt off."

I took my shirt off, and she got a pajama top for me. I put it on (all by myself). "I'll be better tomorrow."

"Look at me, Daphne … You listening?"

"Mhmm."

"If you need to be worse tomorrow, go right ahead, and we'll deal with that together, too. You know that?"

"Mhmm."

"But I hope you have a better day tomorrow, and a better one the day after that, the first step of which is a full night's sleep. Under the covers, little girl. I'll get you some water and be close behind, okay."

"Okay. Thanks for taking care of me. I love you."

"I love you, too. Close those eyes."

Chapter 3: People Are Calling These Gamer Pants Now?

Mom always complains – every single year – that I'm bad at telling her what I want for Christmas. I interpret this as a sign of a financially secure adulthood: if I really want something, I get it. I'm not nine and penniless and waiting for my birthday and Christmas to get a toy I want. Naturally, there are rules, like the one that neither of us spends more than one hundred dollars on a non–necessity without discussing it, and sure, my track record with following that rule is perfect (in its imperfection). But by and large (whatever that means) if I want something, I get it by and by (whatever that means) whether I have to save a little for it or not, so come Christmas and Mom asks me what I want, I'm usually not so much with the ideas. And this year, with me being unemployed and the pandemic pandemicing, what was I gonna ask for? Clothes to wear the office? A new skirt for when I take my vacation to the kitchen?

But Mom also insists you have to have something to open on Christmas. Doesn't matter what it is, but you have to have something wrapped in a box, something tangible. I like that. I think that's right. But my real present from my parents for the past few years has been money. I got the presents to unwrap, and a little belatedly while my parents spent three weeks figuring out Venmo (boomers, amiright?), money.

And what did I spend my money on and didn't even have to consult with Mary because Christmas money is exempt from the rules (but I told her anyway cuz I'm sweet like that)? My very own Xbox. And I know there's a new generation of systems coming out, but I grew up with Xbox and I didn't wanna wait for the new one or spend more, so I ordered my Xbox, waited patiently for several whole days to pass, and when it arrived I went, "Squeeeeeee!"

After all, Mary did say I should get some toys to keep me busy. Pretty sure she meant crafts like needlepoint, but she said toys, so I got a toy.

You may have noticed from the time at Jane's house that I like winning and I like rubbing people's faces in it, and if people are gonna talk smack I'm gonna talk smack, too. I'm nicer about it and less crude than others, but still gonna talk some smack. It's kinda part of the gaming culture, least from where I was sitting. I was getting better, too (at the game, not the smack talk). I don't play a lot and it took some time to get my mojo going because it's one thing to beat Jane and another to beat the obsessives who do nothing but play, and I was starting to get some flow back and not just get owned like a noob (which I am not; I'm just rusty).

So there I was, winning a little after some very frustrating hours and Mary just appeared in front of the screen with her hands on her hips and I leaned left and right trying to see around her and told her, "Mary, you're gonna make me dammit!" I died.

"Daphne Ann, who do you think you are?"

That is such a silly question. She answered it herself – I'm Daphne Ann!

"Me. I'm gonna dammit!" Sure, I coulda paused but, "Dammit! Marrrry!"

"Do you even hear the words that are coming out of your mouth?"

"Some of 'em. Can we dammit!"

"Daphne, look up here," Mary gestured to her face. *Ruh–roh, not a happy face.*

"Sorry. But it's not like I was swearing. I just …"

"Called someone a 'butt mud muncher?' Or are you more sorry for calling someone a 'pie–faced nut knoodler?'"

"Um … least I was creative? You should hear what the other players are saying."

"Are they being a bad influence? Because if they are I will take away your headset."

"But … no, they're not."

Mary sighed. "Okay. So if they're not being a bad influence, then I guess you have no one else to blame your potty mouth on, do you?"

I swear she just pretends to go to work every day in that office. She's really just sitting in there thinking of trip wires to plant. I looked behind me and sure enough, there was the wire, and at the end of it was a pin and tumbling out of a well–camouflaged MRE box was a paddle. I mean, not really, but might as well be. I just decided to sigh instead of say anything in response.

"Little girl, I asked you a question." Deciding not to answer doesn't always work. It's got a track record of about one in five, coincidentally about how I was going on screen before Mary stepped in front of it (progress, people, not perfection).

"I'm not a little girl! I'm just playing like everyone else. It's part of the game."

"Do I need to get you nicer games that aren't rated M?"

"I'm thirty–one years old, and since when do you care if I say stuff like …"

"'Cheese weasel?'"

"What's the problem with 'cheese weasel?'" It was one of the nicer things I said.

"Nothing is wrong when you say it, but you don't say mean things to other people?"

"Mary, you're being …"

"No, you are not being a nice little girl, and I have taught you how to be nice and treat people with kindness, haven't I?"

Okay, change in tactics – maybe if I just let her do whatever it is she wants to do to me I can go back to playing, I thought. "No. I'm sorry."

"Little girls don't use that kind of language. I have half a mind to put you over my knee and spank your bottom. Is that what you want?"

Well, maybe in a few hours around bedtime, but, "No."

"Or how about I wash your mouth out with soap?"

"No, please?" Never again! I hope anyway, but, well, a forlorn hope.

"Not this time, but consider this Strike Two."

"What happened to Strike One," I asked a smidge – a touch, at most – too indignantly.

"You already know better than to name call, young lady. That's your Strike One. Now, up."

"Buh," I started to say before getting up, "I thought I wasn't getting a spanking," I whined.

"O my god, Daphne Ann. Just o. My. God."

"What," I didn't whine.

"Your whining right now. Is this how you get when you play video games?"

"But I was losing and then I finally started to win and I'm thirty–one. I can choose my own words." Which is when Mary folded her arms and gave me her you–can–what–now look. "Um, what I meant so say was, um, when you let me. Love you."

"Floor, missy."

"Aww, please?"

"Fuh–loor."

"Stupid diapers," I muttered as I got down on the fuh–loor. Looking back on it, I'm kinda amazed I didn't get my butt paddled. Mary got the basket out and was next to me in a heartbeat.

"Big girls wear pants," she said as she took my leggings down.

"I am, too, a big girl!"

"Daphne," she said as she paused and looked at me with her what–I'm–about–to–say–is–meaningful look, "you will never be big enough to call people names, and to remind you of that…" She reached into the basket, and before I could fight-or-flee, rubber nipple.

"No! I don't wuk wat." *Stupid pacifier.*

"You'll keep that paci in until dinner time. If I see it out for anything more than drink, you'll keep it in until morning. Understood?"

"Wuhs." *Stupid pacifier!*

"You go right ahead and cross those arms if you wanna pout," she said as I got into my pouting posture. "Doesn't change the fact that you're a piddle pants."

"Umnuhtapudlepunts!"

She fixed me with her you–are–if–I–say–you–are glare. "Yes, you are, until morning, and I'm not kidding Daphne. If this is the kinda mood your new toy is going to put you in, I will take it away."

Ugh! No fair! I was only grumpy because I spent the whole morning getting poned. Do people still say poned? And as soon as I started to get good again, blam! Mary and her rules about not calling people names. It's all part of the game! AND I AM NOT A PIDDLE PANTS!!! Really! (No, REALLY!!!)

"Lift your bottom." Which I did, even though it's not a bottom. It's an ass. I'm not one for crude language, but it's an ass. I'm old enough to call it an ass! Apparently I'm just not old enough to call other people asses. Which isn't the worst rule ever.

"There," she said as she sealed the tapes. *What, no cream?!? That's the good part with the hands and the rubbing and the o it tickles me (glayven). What a rip off.* But then, it was a punishment. Those can't all be fun, I guess.

"Up," she said and held out her hands to help. I can sit up on my own, too, because I'm not a little girl even if she does make me follow rules and wear a stupid diaper. "Such a sour face. Do you need a nap?"

"Nuh."

"You're not the only little girl who needs naps. In fact, most little girls who need diapers take naps."

"(High pitched objections) und (general agitation) und (muffled curses and epithets) und I doh eed iapers!" Would have been a lot more effective and probably wouldn't have made Mary burst out laughing if I hadn't finished my protest by poking my paci back in my mouth before it fell out and I learned about whatever she had acquired to make me sleep with it in.

"Such a cutie patootie!"

"Hmmph!"

"Especially when you're blushing from head to toe."

"M nut!"

"I'm gonna call that Strike two–and–half, Daffodil. I think you'd better cheer up unless you want a smack bottom and an early bedtime."

"(Mumble)."

"What was that?"

"Fuhn."

"I'm going to choose to believe you said 'fine,' and I have work to get back to. You play nicely with your friends, and no more name calling."

Stupid forehead kisses that make me feel so adored and well cared for. Sigh ...

I got back on the couch ready to resume kicking some butt and put my headset back on to hear, "When do you think she's gonna realize the headset picked all that up?"

"MMMMMMMRRRRRRRRRYYYYYY!"

"Serves you right for being a piddle pants."

"And a little girl"

"I'M NOT A LITTLE GIRL!"

"But you are a piddle pants," some meanie head 'asked.'

"Is your pacifier out," I heard from down the hall.

"(Silence)."

Well, Mary heard silence. I heard a bunch of butt faces laughing at me.

Stupid humiliation fetish with the things happening in the pants except I'm not wearing pants and ... time for a ten–minute break.

Chapter 4: I Need More Friends

"I'm sorry I can't come over," Nana said. She didn't need to apologize. I get it – she needed to make a pandemic bubble, and it made more sense for her to do it with her kids and grandkids than us. Makes total sense. Doesn't keep us from talking on the phone though. If it wasn't raining, we'd be talking over the fence.

"That's okay," I told her. "You don't have to apologize every time we talk. Are you keeping busy?"

"It's amazing how many things we can find to do if we just make them up. Are you staying outta trouble?"

Why's she gotta ask questions like that? Loaded question, too. "No more trouble than I can handle," I answered with bravado. Maybe even a little braggadocio. And a touch of bravura.

"Mine always got in trouble on rainy days."

"Your what, Nana? You never had one of me." Which came out without me really meaning for it to. It's just that she says stuff like that sometimes, and I always think the same thing: she never had one of me.

"Sorry. You know what I mean."

"I'm not a little girl." Ooo, turns out I was in a snippy mood. Wish I'd known that before I called.

"I know. I'm sorry. I just …"

"No, I'm sorry. I didn't mean to be snippy. Just that I'm … blegh." I'm blegh. The whole world is blegh, and as world leader, I'm blegh, too, both because I am and because I have blegh constituents' blegh-ness to represent.

"Light at the end of tunnel, though. Do you know when you might get a vaccine? You're prioritized, aren't you?"

"I have no idea. My immunologist says she doesn't know anything. I can't believe no one even has a plan … I wanna drink now."

"It's nine–thirty."

"I know. Getting a late start."

"Ha! Tell me about your vacation instead. You still haven't."

"It was good. Fine."

"You told me that part already, silly. What did you guys do for a whole week?"

What did we do for a whole week? Well, here's how I've pieced it together in my head: we went on vacation; the break in the routine made me forget about COVID for just long enough for me to forget my mask; I totally freaked myself out and had a meltdown.

"We just social distanced elsewhere. We went snowshoeing … There was a sauna."

"I hope you had more fun than that. Was it at least nice to get away from the house for a bit?"

"Yeah. It was." That part was good. "It was a nice break … Hard to come back."

"I'm sure."

"How's your family?"

Well, that wasn't our best conversation. There really isn't anyone to talk to during the (increasingly long) days. Mary, obviously, but all my other friends are working. Maybe if I had kids, I'd have some stay–at–home mom friends, and then I'd be a stay–at–home mom, too, instead of unemployed and lonely. We could use some more friends anyway. Normal ones we've never seen naked and who have never touched my butt. Don't get me wrong, I like our friends, and we do have some vanilla friends, but all our close friends are from the scene.

I did go to college out here. You'd think I'd have some friends from back then who were still here. Or anywhere. Who goes to college and doesn't have any college friends?

And work friends are really important to have, but not many make that transition to outside–of–work friends. I had none of those. Not anymore their fault than my fault. Just the way it is. End of the workday, and everyone just wanted to go home. Weekends, and you just don't want to be thinking about work. That line between the two is good, or it seemed so back then. It went work–line–home. I hated office social events, too.

My awkward was always on full blast, or so it seemed to me (I've been told I'm a terrible judge of that), and then I spent way too much time thinking about this or that thing I'd said. And it always just seemed weird to think of interacting with someone outside the setting I was used to knowing them in. Weirder, when you think about it, that you can see someone every workday for years and then one day never again. Something so artificial about work relationships. Or at least I think there must be if it's so easy to just cast one aside.

No one ever teaches you how to make friends as an adult. People help you make friends when you're a kid. Being a kid just comes with all sorts of ways to make friends, too. School, sports, activities, clubs. And groups, too. How do you be part of a group as an adult? Wish someone had told me at my last track meet that it wasn't only my last track meet but my last time ever being part a team. And work is not a team. People can call it that, but a team is something you join because you want to, not because you have to or you won't be able to eat. Still, it was good having common purpose.

But Mary can do it. She's made new friends as an adult. Mostly as part of the scene, but not only. She can do almost anything, but I gotta remind myself that's just the way it seems from where I sit. There are lots of people like Mary (but only one actual Mary). How come people like that can make new friends, but not me? What do they know that I don't? How are they different?

Truthfully, I wasn't very good at making friends as a kid either. I was monogamous in my friendships, so to speak. I had my handpicked circle, and I really didn't like it when one of them would try to add someone. They were interlopers. I was jealous and protective. I didn't like that my friends had friends outside our circle, which was odd because I was friends with some really popular people, and I was decently popular too. Just in a more distant way. Two of my friends thought I had social anxiety, and I did. I just didn't like new people.

Not like I mean to be that way, and I didn't like being that way then either. Even now, I'm not a big fan of new people coming into our friend groups. How screwed up are people that even when we want more connections, we don't want to actually meet people or let them in? We're more worried about losing what we have, even when there's no risk of it, than afraid of missing out on what we might gain.

And how screwed up is it that who we are at age five is pretty much who we are at thirty–one? They say you get less neurotic with age but that your personality is pretty much your personality forever. I hope not. *Sigh…*

I knocked on Mary's office door. "You busy?"

"I can take a break. What's up?"

"I'm lonely. Wanna make lunch together?"

"It's only ten."

"I'm stress eating again," I confessed. All I want anymore is sugar and fat. I had seven meals yesterday. Eight if you count the cosmo I kept topped up from early afternoon through bedtime.

"How about some fruit," Mary suggested as she got up from her chair and glanced at her phone before putting it in her pocket. As if we we weren't all attached to those things too much already before the pandemic.

"Kay … Can I put peanut butter on it?"

"A little bit, silly goose."

"I'm not a silly goose," I said all plaintively and goose-like as I started toward the kitchen. "I just like peanut butter."

"Hey," Mary said and grabbed my wrist gently. I turned around, and she put her hand under my chin to lift my gaze to hers. "You feeling okay?"

"I'm just … blegh."

"Let's be blegh together then."

"Kay."

It's better being blegh with someone than being blegh alone.

Chapter 5: A Lesson in Ladylike Hygiene

"O, Daffy," my dearest wife called out. "O, Daffodilio," she added because she is such a Flanders. Seriously.

"Yep," I replied as I passed through our bedroom to the master bath. Kinda weird when you think about that term. 'Master bedroom'? I can guess where it came from, but it makes it sound like some command–and–control center from which Captain Mary flies our house. Which reminds me of this Halloween when she dressed up as a naval officer and tied me to the yardarm and launched a thousand ships. Or possibly one ship a thousand times. I was distracted by ... a thing.

Anyhoo, she was sitting on the edge of the tub wearing her fancy robe, the one reserved for ... never. It mostly stays in the closet. And she was swirling her fingers in the warm water, being all tempting.

"C'mere," she said to me.

I thought of the coolest, sexiest thing to say as I glided across the rug like the sylph–like creature that I am, and I made my sultry face and said, "Ha!" (I know, but it came sexier than it sounds).

She smiled her Daphne–is–so–suave smile, which to the untrained eye looks like her Daphne–is–such–a–goofy–doofy smile, but trust me. Not the case. (Really). In fact, so overtaken with my wiles was she that she didn't even say anything. She just reached out and took my shorts down, leaving me in my sexy–to–the–point–of–sultry (Muppet–print) panties (dammit). And then they joined my sweatpants (sexy sweatpants – really) at my ankles.

I started to take my shirt off and got, "Ah–ah–ah. Let me do that. Arms up." Which I did, and then I was naked. Know what's fun? Being naked with Mary. It's fun when she's naked, too, and it's fun when she's wearing clothes because I like feeling all vulnerable and smol and stuff. Maybe she needs a suit of armor so she can be a shiny knight and I can be the naked nymph who won't let her inside my ... tree house (I guess?) unless she guesses my riddles three (the answers are, in no particular order, "I", "Said", and "Now." But don't go blabbing it to her. Gotta make her work a little, amiright?)

"How is it," Mary said, "that a little girl who spent the whole day inside can get so dirty?"

"Am not," I didn't pout despite what you may hear in the form of lies from lying liars who tell lies when they're lying (really!).

"So dirty," Mary said and took my hand and 'helped' me into the tub. "Close your eyes," she said and poured a pitcher of warm water over my head.

"Mmmm. What made you decide to do this?"

"I figured you're getting to be a woman Daphne, and it's time I teach you a few things."

Which is when I made my so–not–impressed–with–your–snark face. She snarks at a ninth grade–level, max. I have a doctorate of snark in snark. The day I was born, the doctor slapped me on the ass, took one look at my ear–to–ear grin and said, "She's gonna be a snarky one." That's right – diagnosed snarky!

"Now," Mary said while trying to snark and failing (fuh–ail–ing), "with this womanly figure you're developing come certain responsibilities, such as," she trailed off and picked up a razor. "I know it's winter and you're not going out, but I think maybe it's time for you to learn how to shave your legs."

And for the record (we're creating more records than the Beatles and the court of the Han dynasty combined, people!) I wasn't blushing. It was just a hot bath.

"I get your point," I said and held out my hand for the razor.

"Silly goose, like I'm gonna trust you with a razor when you've barely graduated out of your training bra."

"Bitch!" Not sure if she heard me over the splash. If you're gonna make funna someone in the bathtub, you're gonna get splashed. That's just physics. And her silky robe was suddenly clinging to her ... hmmm.

"Daphne Ann," she said while wiping her brow off (don't worry – most of the water got stopped by the floor), "just because you're old enough to shave your legs doesn't mean you're too old for a spanking, and with that kind of language you better believe you're getting a wet–bottom spanking."

So she did hear that.

"You're being so mean." I would never tell her to shave her legs more often. In part because she does it more often than me and in part because I would get paddled like a canoe. But then stubbly legs aren't so fun and I do sort wrap myself around her a lot.

"This isn't about body shaming, Daphne. It's about teaching you about all the ways your body is changing."

Ya know what? Fine. I can play along. I can keep up. *I am, too, a big girl!* In fact, the biggest (that doesn't sound right). In fact, an actual adult! But I can play her game better than she can, so I said, "You mean changes like how I'm having these strange, new feelings when I watch you get undressed before bed?"

Also, when she looks all studious while she's working, and when she smiles at me, and when she scolds me, and when she says embarrassing stuff about me, and when she licks the spoon when the ice cream is all gone, and when she tells me I'm pretty and a good girl (weak knees, for realzies), and when I catch a glimpse of her wedding ring that says she's all mine.

But about her teaching me about these strange, new (for many years) feelings... "Sure. Also," she said like she wasn't cracking up inside, "I'll teach you how around this time in a young woman's life they should start wearing deodorant."

"Such a B," I said and folded my arms and then unfolded them because it sent the wrong message and to clear it up, I had to add, "I do, and you know it." She doesn't inspire any feelings at all, so I made my indifferent face.

"No need to pout." I wasn't pouting (really!). "Gimme a footsie."

"No."

"No?"

"You're gonna tickle it." I'm on to her.

"Such a silly goose. That would just get more water on the floor. Footsie."

"Fine." I put my heel on the rim of the tub. "Ya know," I said trying to turn things to my advantage, "if I earned a bedtime spanking, don't you think it's only right that I suffer a bedtime orgasm as well?"

"You already had one today."

"Did not!"

"I heard you!"

"O, yeah, that. ... But that doesn't even count because you weren't there. We should do things together as wife and wife. Perverse things. Butt things even." I tried to wink, but I think that's genetic or something because I just blinked.

"What was that?"

"I winked."

"Looked like a ministroke," she laughed and rubbed slippery stuff on my leg. I liked that part.

"Is it Tease Daphne Day?" What stupid ass munching jerkoffasaurus head of marketing invented that day?

"Every day is Tease Daphne Day, and like you don't like it."

"Nuh–uh!"

"Uh–huh."

"O, Mary, that was just so beneath you."

"Ha! Well, I can tell when you like stuff. I'm good at that."

"How can you tell?" I know how she can tell. I just wanted to hear her list the things. Also, I don't like it (really!).

"The little red spot on your collar bone."

"Other ways?"

"The blush in your cheeks."

"The water is hot!"

"The way you don't know what do to with your hands."

"I'm naked and wet and vulnerable. What the heck am I supposed to do with my hands?"

"Modest young ladies would cover their princess parts."

"I am modest! ... And a lady! ... And a princess! I'm lots of things, ya know. Things you don't even know about."

"Daphne, I've seen you inside and out." True story, not gonna tell it, never playing with med fet toys again ... probably. "I don't think there's many secrets about your little body I don't know. All done! Gimme your other footsie." Which I did because I'm averse to conflict, not because she's the boss of me.

"O yeah," I challenged her. "If you know so much about my body, what does it mean when the little button gets all red and big?"

"I'll tell you when you're mature enough to be trusted with a vibrator unsupervised."

"And if I confess I've been using one unsupervised going on about fifteen years, will you teach me about butt stuff? And is it true the safest way to use a lifelike dildo is to strap it to your wife?"

"I love it when you get embarrassed and try to cover it by being dirty and hypersexual. Does talking like a big girl make you feel more grown up?"

"I ... Stop calling me out." It's not polite to be calling people out on all their things.

"There. See how nice and smooth? Doesn't that feel good?"

"My leg, or you rubbing my leg?"

"And after I show you a few more times, you can try. Under my supervision, naturally. Isn't that exciting?"

"(Glaring)."

"Maybe just once a month to get started. That's more frequent than now, right," she asked because she's a smartass. There's a difference between smartassery and snarkiness, and the latter is superior in every way.

"No!" I'm not an Amazon. I'm very delicate and ladylike. But it's long pants season. Once a week is fine.

"And it will have the added bonus of feeling so much nicer on my thighs when you're squirming around over my knee for your latest naughty behavior."

"Is that ... really?" So that's how she noticed. But as much as I (and every woman who is normal) hate that chore, I don't mind it so much if she does it.

"Really. And speaking of which, you need a wet–bottom spanking for that language and the splashing. Stand up."

"But you were being mean to me. You were body shaming, is what you were doing. That's very toxic." Not the thinnest of arguments, not the not thinnest.

"I was helping you with your hygiene and teaching you about what happens when little girls grow up."

"Grr."

She made her I'm–having–a–fake–realization face. "Is your little tantrum your way of telling me you're not ready be a big girl?"

"Keep talking. I'll just be under the water." Where it's peaceful and no one teases me.

"There's that spot on your collar bone again."

"Stop pointing out my spots!"

"I'm just saying, Daphne, not being ready to be a grown up would be a perfectly good excuse for that little outburst. That's a big and complicated feeling for such a little girl ... and somewhat to be expected from a girl like you. Graduating to a real bra but still needing 'big girl' diapers sometimes must be very confusing."

Her and her stupid invisible air quotes. "I wish I had a snorkel."

"You wanna get some bath toys?"

"O my god."

"Is that a yes?"

"Yeah, something that squirts, so I can soak you some more."

"I already have a little toy that squirts and gets me wet."

Which is when I made my raccoon–in–the–flashlight eyes. Pupils dilated. The works. Not that I changed my mind from being put out and victimized to wanting to be touched and victimized and played like a lamellophone but did you hear her with the words and the teasing (which I hate) and the humiliating belittlement and implications of my middleness (hate it, really!) and the rubbing my leg and the clingy robe and the words with the double meanings and the confident domineering sexiness and what she implied she wants to do to me?

A travesty is what it is! And I wanted no part of it (even if I wanted all the parts of it – really!).

"Buh..." I said all suavely (really), "If I take my spanking like a good girl, will you show me how to play with your little toy?" I like toys. I wanna learn all the games. I'm a good sport. As gracious in victory as I am in defeat, and not to blow my own horn but I'm never lost at horn blowing.

And she of the world conquering confidence who totally conquered my world but was all benevolent, though firm, about it said, "If you promise to hold extra still and not splash while I'm spanking your bottom. Do you promise me?"

"Muh–huh." *Daffies make the best bath toys*, I thought to myself as I got to my feet and turned toward the wall and stuck out my butt because I'm not only a good girl but a great girl. The best, really, but I'm too polite and humble to say so. Really.

"And then when you're tuckered out from play time and too weak and blissed out to resist, we'll get you in your nighttime diaper."

"I'm getting cold. Could we get with the spanking?"

"And don't you feel bad about it. I'm sure you'll be dry at night before you start college in the fall, and even if you're not, I have a feeling your roommate won't mind."

"This is cutting into playtime," I said to whatever she was yammering on about. Something about the stock market? Yada yada exchange trade funds yada. Amiright?

"Little girl, you hold real still," she said and grabbed a handful of butt and squeezed (so very very) hard and put her hand on ... Not sure what it's called. My mind went blank with the feelings and the sensation and the o it feels good on me (hoyven).

Maybe I do need some remedial lessons in princess parts and how they work. And learning by doing is fun.

(But I do shave my legs often enough and wear deodorant every day. Really!)

Chapter 6: Once Upon a Time

"What are you thinking about," Mary asked me. She's the type of person who looks at another person and wonders what she's thinking about, mostly cuz she likes me and stuff. She wants to know what's going on with me at all the times.

As for me, I'm the type of person who wants to lay across Mary's lap because it's one of my happy places. Sorta like how a kitten, which Mary keeps calling me lately, likes to lay across the top of the couch.

So what was I thinking about? This one time, maybe six months after we started dating. *(Insert harp music here).*

The year was 2014(ish), and the country was obsessed with this show called Game of Thrones. So obsessed that we were having a watch party with some of Mary's friends, and I was enjoying the terrific sense of superiority that came with having read the books. Knowing the future was intoxicating, as was the cabernet. At 9% alcohol by volume, I was tipsy after the first glass because I'm a world–class drinker, and when I drink I become uncharacteristically talkative. Normally I'm so laconic. People say, *There goes Daphne. She's so laconic.* Really. And yet being talkative and knowing what happens and being excited led me to (spoiler alert) let slip a spoiler. Some guests were, as the saying goes, displeased, as was Mary.

I have this thing – call it a good upbringing – that says never to fight in front of company. Mary has this thing – call it an evil streak – that goes, "We're not fighting. You're in trouble, and I don't care if we have company."

"It was an accident, though."

"You talked through most of the show even after I asked you watch quietly, and you blurted out the ending. That was very rude to our guests."

"Can we talk about this privately," I asked again while trying and failing to not look at the guests in question. Some looked satisfied to see me get lectured, and some looked delighted to see get lectured. It was then that I realized I needed a vanilla friend to invite to stuff so Mary couldn't chastise me in front of people. This wasn't even a play party. And I still hardly knew these people. I could still count on one hand the number of times Mary had actually chastised me outside a scene and the number of times Mary had done what I was pretty sure she was about to do in front of these people was a big fat zero.

"Daphne Ann," she said. And did anyone else notice the very first question she ever asked me was my middle name? She had designs on me, as evidenced by yanking me over her knee the first moment she ever saw me, but that was at a play party. "Are you a girl who gets spanked?"

"Marrrrry," I said quietly. "You're embarrassing me."

"I asked you a question. Are you a girl who gets spanked?"

"Yes," I whispered.

"I'm sorry?"

"Yes! This is so ..."

"That's right. You're a spanked girl now, and you're getting a spanking right now."

"No! You can't!"

"Do you think these people don't know what happens to naughty girls who get spankings? Do you want to ask what they think?"

"It's eleven o'clock. Can't they just leave?"

"They can leave when they're ready. Over my knee."

"No, please?"

"Is that a hard no?"

O sweet baby jebus was I conflicted on that. It's not like I hadn't been spanked in front of people before, and even some of the guests. It's just that I hadn't ever been actually punished in front of other people before. And Mary was being (wistful sigh) something I had wanted for a long time, someone willing to take me in hand. Lots of people had said they wanted to, but Mary was the first to actually get what it meant and to follow through. I liked what was happening, I hated what was happening, and I so wanted to obey and run away all at the same time. But damn did I not want an audience. I was flushed and blushing head to toe and these butterflies were flapping their flippers in my tummy.

"No," I said, "but this isn't even a big deal. Can't we just …"

"No we can't." And suddenly I was face down over Mary's knee looking at the carpet. If I turned and looked toward my feet, I could see all of our guests upside down. Fitting metaphor for the state of affairs, somehow (sort of? Not really). "Why are you over my knee about to get your bottom spanked?"

"Because I spoiled the ending and kept talking when you told me not to."

"Disobeying is a big deal, Daphne. You need to make better choices, and when you make a bad choice, you're going to get your bottom spanked every single time. I don't care where we are or who's there. I'll drop your pants in front of everybody. That's what happens to spanked girls like you. Understood?"

O, just get the friggin' frack on with it. "Yes."

"You're going to make a good choice right now and not fight me on this, aren't you?"

"Yes."

"Brenna will be only too happy to help me if you can't hold still." *Smack ... smack ... smack*

My god can she talk. At least she left my pants up. Stupid butterflies in my tummy. Just calm down. You've been here before. It's not even like you did anything so wrong. It'll be over in thirty seconds.

(Smack smack smack smack smack)

See, it does even hurt (SMACK!) that much. She's just showing off – ow – for her friends. Ow. Some of whom are cute. Ow ow. Even Brenna ow in a big kinda way ow ow. She's getting a little enthusiastic up there. OW! Geez, it wasn't even the penultimate ep–OUCH! Dammit.

"I think these can come down," Mary said as she tugged my pants down to my knees!

"Hey! I didn't say OW!"

"This is a punishment, Daphne Ann. Spanked girls don't get to decide how they get spanked, and if you think (SMACK!) you're (SMACK!) getting out of this (SMACK SMACK SMACK!) with your (SMACK!) undies up (SMACK!) you have got (SMACK!) another thing coming."

"You wouldn't dare!" In retrospect, I realize now how that statement can be interpreted as a challenge that sorta backs someone into a corner. At the time, my immediate thought after letting that bon mot come out of my mouth was, *Holy fuck she dared!* Because down my panties instantly came. Later on, as I was nursing a sore butt at work the next day, I began to suspect I was dating a ninja because I don't know she got those down in the first place.

"O yes I will dare," was Mary's response when she just as well could've said *o yes I did.*

My calm, collected manner – you know, the way I'm always level–headed and rational and take things in a very laid back manner – disappeared. I mean, I am all those things. I used to be all those things. I used to be all those things and still am all those things and then Mary came along and still I am those things. Well, not in that moment which went something like, "Mary! Stop! Lemme go! OW! Ow! That hurt! Lemme go! OW! OW! EEP! EEE! OUCH!"

And the team of little people inside my head who are in charge of the kinesiology department said, *Break right! Try left! Kick the feet! Arch the back! Break right again! Squinch the eyes shut! Pound the floor! Try left again! Grab the chair legs! Try to pull forward! Kick the legs! Once more with feeling!*

I would so fire those people if I could. Not once did they say, o, I dunno, *Keep the legs shut! Everybody can see everything!*

"Hold (SMACK!) still (SMACK!) like a (SMACK!) good (SMACK!) girl!"

"I am so mad at you," was my response. I mean, it made sense for me to say so, when you think about it. It was a very opportune time to talk about feelings because it's always a good time to talk about our feelings. Mr. Rogers, who was played by Tom Hanks himself in the biopic (so you know he was either really important or had something terrible happen to him on a plane), said so. For a split second, I thought Mary agreed, but nope. Nope, she was just putting her leg over mine.

"Brenna, would you please go get the paddle in the kitchen drawer under the silverware?"

"Don't you dare!"

"Don't you talk to our guests that way, young lady! I don't know (SMACK!) what (SMACK!) has gotten into you (SMACK!)."

This isn't fun this isn't fun this isn't fun OW! OWIE! "OWIE!" *O my god I said owie. Who even says that?* "Mary this isn't OWWW!"

"This is a punishment, Daphne Ann."

"All I did was spoil the ending."

"You disobeyed – thank you, Brenna. (CRACK!)"

"Aaaah!"

"Spanked girls (CRACK!) stop (CRACK!) when they are told (CRACK!) to (CRACK!) stop."

"(Sniff!)" *What the fuck is this wetness in my eyes? That's not supposed to be there. I've taken so much worse than this without so much as a meep. Am I crying? What the hell? She made me cry? What a bitch!*

"Ow! Ah! Ah–ha! Eh–heh! Eh–heh! Eh–heh!" *O you are not going to start sobbing like some wimpy little girl.* "Wahhhh!" *Hey. Hey, shut up! You're embarrassing yourself. Stop. Please stop?* "Waaah ah! OW! Ah–haaaaaaa! Wahhhh–haaaaah!" *Fine, go ahead a cry.*

So I did. And did some more even after Mary stopped paddling me.

"Shhh. Deep breaths, baby."

And I did that thing where your diaphragm cramps and you just suck in air, which goes, "Hhhhh!"

"Calm down, deep breaths. There's my good girl. Can you sit up for me? C'mon."

Everything was blurry with the tears for the split second between picking my head up and burying my face in Mary's chest. O, I like it there so much. I don't think I'm safer anywhere else than with my face pressed into Mary's chest with my eyes shut tight and her arms all around me and her hands rubbing my back and teasing my hair and her lips making soft, quiet kisses on me.

I stayed just like that while everyone filed out (not that I was paying much attention), which is what you do when a scene ends so that the bottom can get their aftercare. Or in my case so the naughty spoiler can get her aftercare.

"Good girl," Mary kept cooing at me. "Such a good girl. I know that was very hard."

"(Meep. Sniff. Inward sob.)"

"I'm so proud of you."

"I'm sorry for being bad."

"No, sweetheart, you weren't bad. You just made a bad choice. You're always my good girl." O, god, was that an arrow through my bleeding heart.

"Ahhh–haaaaaa–haa–haahhh! (Sobbing wookie noise) (Moose with a cold) (Elephant snorting water)."

"Shh shhh shhhh shh. Dry up those tears."

"Imrying." That would be *trying*, for all those who don't speak sobbing Daphne, which Mary didn't yet. We'd only been together six months, and I wasn't always a crybaby. And I'm not a crybaby now. Really.

"I know you're crying sweetie. You're doing it on my shirt," she said with a chuckle.

"I said 'I'm trying.' (sniff)."

"Can we talk a little bit now?"

"Mhmm."

"I'm sorry I had to spank you, but you need to make good choices and listen when I tell you things. I know you're new at being a submissive, but that's part of what it means, and as your domme I'm going to hold you to that. Does that make sense?"

"Yes. I'm sorry."

"I know, and you're all forgiven. You got your consequence, and it's over, but you're gonna feel that sore bottom as a reminder."

"But did you hafta do it front of them?"

"I give the spankings, and you're the girl who gets spanked. If we're with kinky company, I will spank your bottom if you need a spanking right then, and you did spoil the show for them."

"But they saw."

"They've all seen girls get spanked before, and what they saw was a girl who needed a spanking. But, and listen carefully to me, did you want to red light and didn't?"

"No ... sort of."

"Which one?"

"No." I did and didn't, and then when she bared me and everyone could see ... it didn't even occur to me to red light then. I pretty much spent the week trying to figure that out. All I could come up with is that it didn't seem like an option. It was, and I knew that, but it didn't seem like an option because, just like Mary said, spanked girls don't get to decide when or how they get their butts spanked. Even if they don't want a spanking, they get one. Mary decides. Mary decided. "No," I repeated. I liked that Mary decided. I wanted her to decide even if I didn't like her decision.

"I'm very happy to hear that. I don't ever want you to do anything you don't want to. Will you promise me you won't?"

"I promise," I said in my please–don't–make–me–cry–again voice.

"That's my good girl. And I'm proud of you for obeying and being brave. You were very brave."

"I sobbed."

"That's okay. It's okay to cry when you get spanked."

"But I don't, normally. You know." Trust me, she knew. She'd spanked me lots of ways. She'd spanked me way harder than that for playtime, and spanked me for punishment (maybe twenty percent funishment), but she had never spanked me that hard for punishment. That's when I put two and two together and came up with the equation *in trouble with Mary plus hard spanking equals I cry like my puppy died*.

"It's okay to cry, especially when you're having big feelings and getting a big spanking. I know how brave you are. I won't ever think less of you if you need to cry."

"I know. I just ... everybody saw."

"Are we still on that, silly goose?"

"What?"

"Still on everybody seeing."

"No, what did you call me?"

"A silly goose."

"I am not a silly goose," I said while putting my face back on the driest part of her shirt I could find.

"Said my silly goose. And you know something else? I may be strict with you, but it's only because I love you and want what's best for you."

Which is when my face came off her chest in a hurry and I made great big eyes at her. (And geese have tiny eyes; I am not a silly goose. Really!)

"Mary, is that, um, are you saying that because headspace or …"

"I'm saying Daphne, that I will spank your bottom wherever and whenever and hold you until you stop crying and do anything else you ever need because I love you very much."

"I love you too." O, she can hug so good with the kisses and the caressing.

"I think we should go wash that pretty face of yours, and then it's bedtime, and I call big spoon."

"You're always the big spoon." Well, almost.

"C'mon," she said and took me by the hand.

"Mary?"

"Yeah?"

"Love you. Oooo, that feels so good."

"Such a silly goose. And I love you, too."

(Insert harp music here)

So I told Mary, "I was thinking about you."

"What about?"

"How much I like you."

"Just like me?"

"And love you lots."

"And I love you muchly."

We're disgustingly cute when we're not being disgustingly filthy. Really. (No, really).

Chapter 7: More Fun for Mary than Me, Um, Really

"Daffodil," someone sang. "Daffodil."

"Govay," was my response. There may have been little foot kicks, but my heart wasn't in them.

"It's time to get up."

"It's Saturday."

"Don't you wanna get up and play with me? You're gonna make me sad."

"Everyone needs to learn to deal with adversity (yawn)." And did I mention that not having access to me really is an adverse event? Really. And then I pulled the covers over my head. And then I ordered her out of our room with a stinging, "Muhsubuhbuh (snore)."

Which was followed by a wooshing sensation as she yanked the covers off me, leaving me cold and naked (up top) and indignant. "Marrrrry," I throatily groaned. I didn't whine (I never whine – really). It was the same type of groan one might hear from an irritable Viking right before they heft their battle axe (the kind as big as me).

To which Mary responded by grabbing my delicate, teeny lady ankles and yanking me to the foot of the bed. Whole lot of yanking going on that morning. There I was, half–naked and none too happy about being forced from my winter night's sleep, with Mary leaning over me with a hand pressed into the bed on either side. Lesser women than me would've felt trapped or at least intimidated, but not me. For I am Daphne – Shieldmaiden and owner of an Amazon Prime account. I wasn't intimidated (really!) even when she leaned all the way down and took a big sniff of my neck like she was a predator smelling prey before she landed these violently gentle love kisses on my neck and cheek and lips one–two–three.

"Are you sure you don't wanna play with me today?"

"That depends. What game are we playing?" Because if she wanted to play Torment Daphne, I've already played it and lost, like, all the times. Which is totally weird given my uninterrupted winning streak in life and the things.

"Does it really matter," she asked and kissed her way down my chest to my tummy with her hair brushing all soft and ticklish down my skin. Ya know something? I like her. I think I'm gonna keep Mary around.

"No," I said as she kiss–kiss–kissed my tummy and her fingers started caressing and tickling and wandering up and down my sides where my skin is very soft and sensitive.

"Goody," Mary said, and I should've been more suspicious than I was because she said it just like the Big Bad Wolf, and I didn't even have my little red hood on. I was about to retract my consent when she, "Pbbbbbt!"

"Mary!"

"Pbbbbt!"

"Heeheehee st– heeeheeheee!"

"Pbbbt!"

"Mary! No raspber– heeheehee!" *Grrr*. "No raspberries!"

"Are you awake now?"

"Yes!"

"Then let's get our day started. What am I gonna find when I pull down these shorts of yours?"

"Princess parts."

"Is that all," she said as she pulled down my pajama shorts. I only wore them to cover …

"What's this? Hmm? Is this a wet diapee?" *Pat–pat–squeeze.* "It is! Did you have an accident last night?"

"Marrrry. It's too early for teasing. Be nice to me."

"I'd never tease you for bedwetting, sweetums."

"I didn't wet the bed," I ferociously squeaked. Why's she gotta say stuff like that?

"It's okay. You're just not ready to be out of diapers at night."

"Marrrry! You're the one who put it on me at 9:00 last night and wouldn't let me take it off." I wasn't wearing a wet diaper. I was wearing fault. Specifically, it was Mary's fault.

She tore open the tapes. "Dere dey are," she said. "There are the princess parts I was promised. Now, up–up."

"Is this part of the game, or are you just being weird again?" I asked as I sat up. Instead of an answer, I got one of her this–will–shut–her–up kisses that makes me go all a–flutter with the lightheadedness and the oxygen deprivation and the tummy tingles (glayven). Hee!

"You gonna be my good girl today?"

"I thought I was your good girl all the time."

"You are, and you're gonna make very good choices for me, aren't you?"

"Muh–huh," was my clever and sexy response to the lust eyes she was making at me. Ya don't think she does that to make me docile and pliable, do you? I don't think so. Really. That's not the kind of person she is, and also because I am not so easily manipulated. For evidence of my iron will, I would point to all the times she's had to coerce me into good choices. Yep, that's me – a brass butt and an iron will.

"Go to the bathroom and call me when you're done."

It was a five–minute trip, if you get my drift. I'm very regular thanks to Mary's nutritional know how. If I had my way, there'd be a lot more Cheetos. Did you know that cat mascot actually has snow-white fur and is just covered in Cheeto dust? Really. I bet it's very bad for his lungs.

Miss Mary Queen of Everything did not wait for me to call her, which I wasn't gonna because why the heck would I? She came in at the flush. Which was very presumptuous. A little mystery in a marriage is a good thing. Not that you need to be Poirot to deduce that particular whodunnit.

"All done," she asked.

"I don't like that question."

"Sit back down."

"Why?"

"O look, did you remember we own a bathbrush?"

O look, I'm sitting. And naked. Yep, sitting and naked (stupid bathbrush X men reject mutant butthead hanging on the bathroom wall).

"Let's see how you did," Mary said. "Open your legs for me … Why are you making your raccoon eyes?"

I had my reasons. She tore off a piece of toilet paper and ,"Good job in the front. Lean forward."

"Mar– EEEEP!"

"And good job in back! Such a good girl."

"Fffpawtuh nurlsen, Mary!"

"Awww, and you're very welcome! And it's so cute when you sputter."

"But buh buh…"

"Up you go. Let's wash our hands."

Washing our hands was a quiet affair. I say washing "our" hands, but really Mary washed my hands and her hands. I like her hands, and I like it when she uses them to wash my hands. But – and stay with me here – WHAT THE FUCKING FUCK WAS FUCKING THAT?

"Daffy," she said to me like the world is a just place, "did you know when you get all blushy and extra special embarrassed the left side of your face kinda sneers?"

That's a mini–stroke. One day my face will freeze that way and it won't be so cute then.

She moved me in front of her and hugged me from behind. "I'm cold," I complained. Funny how you can blush from head to toe and still be cold.

"Brush your toofies and I'll get some clothes out for you."

Just like that, she disappeared into the bedroom leaving me to brush my teeth. Teeth. I do not and never have had toofies. I don't even know what those are. But I will tell you this: your teeth are the best friends you got. If you take care of them, they'll take care of you. But I still didn't wear my retainer after getting my braces off, and my teeth look fine. Thieving orthodontists with their cosmetic procedures dressed up as necessities. Two whole years of caramel lost.

I decided the best thing I could do was saunter into the bedroom like I hadn't a care in the world. That's the way to deal with bullies like Mary, just ignore them. Don't let them know they get under your skin at all. So what if she wiped my butt ... *O gawd I can't believe she did that. Ourgh!!! ... I have to move out of our house now.*

"You brushed your hair."

"Yeah," I said, "I do that every day."

"Come." *I am not a dog,* I said to myself in my head as I walked over to her. "Here," she said and held out ...

"Do I hafta wear a pullup? What's wrong with my panties?"

"They don't absorb anything." Well, I walked into that one, literally, sorta. "And not so long ago you were trying to get me to start putting you back in these."

Lies! Lies and wickedness! "That's ... Mary, you're just so nyegh sometimes."

"You told me you wanted to wear pullups more."

"I told you I wanna wear diapers less."

"That's not what I heard."

"Of course it wasn't," I roared. Sometimes my roars come out like grumbles and muttering. But they're roars. Really.

"Besides, no one goes straight from diapers to pullups."

"I didn't! I ... dammit!" She broke my brain. I was all twitterpated and upside down and inside out and scrambled with the synapses and the transducers and fiberoptics tangled and stuff. "Stop looking so delighted!"

"Did you or did you not wake up in a diaper this morning?"

"You know I did."

"And what condition was it in?"

"Pris–fucking–tine." *And there she goes again with looking all delighted and happy with herself!*

"You're so …"

"Don't say it!"

"Pretty and adorable when you're indignant and in denial."

"I deny that."

"Ha! See?"

"Gimme my shirt," I said and reached around her and put it on. "Where are my pants?" If you're gonna lay out someone's clothes, you gotta lay out the pants. She volunteered for the responsibility; I didn't ask her to. *WHERE ARE MY PANTS!!!*

"No pants today."

"You wake me up. You nyeghed me in the bathroom. You make me wear these things that aren't even mine and are soooo yours. And now I can't have pants?"

"You are so on top of current events. Want some socks?" *Grimace! See my grimace at you and wither!* "Sit down and gimme a feetsie."

"Fine. But only because my toes are cold."

"What else would socks be for, you silly goose."

"I am not a silly goose." Everyone's a silly goose but me. Hmmph! (Except actual geese. They are not silly. They are dead serious and ill-tempered. Really.)

"Do you wanna hear the rules for today," she asked while putting my fuzzy warm socks on.

"If I say no, do I still have to follow them?"

"Yep."

"There's no justice in the world."

"I seem to recall a little girl who once upon a time told me that she wants me to make the rules and decide what is and isn't just."

"She was twenty–six and high on sexcapades." Mary had been doing things to me. Ensorcelling me by making me fall utterly and totally in love with her until I was completely dependent on her opinion of me and wanted nothing so much as to please her and hear her call me a good girl. (I am not a golden retriever – really!)

"The rule today is, you come tell me if you need the potty."

"What do I get in exchange for obeying?"

"Your butt gets to live another day, but," she said and gave me her I'm–about–to–pounce–on–you look right before she (oof!) pounced on me, "don't you wanna be my good girl and play my game today?"

What even is that that she thinks she can just (*mmm*) kiss my neck (*ooo*) and tickle my (*hhhh*) and raise the prospect of me disappointing her (*urgh*) and think she can manipulate me (*grrr*) into her latest depravities (*heehee*)? Where did she even get that idea (other than our history as a couple dating back a significant percentage of our lives)?

So entitled. Unethical. Against nature and the rights of humankind. Well, I had had enough, and I told her right where she could put her manipulations (*fi!*) and coercions (*eep!*) and rewards (*muh*) and tongue (mmm!). I told her off and said, "Yes'm." *Dammit* …

"Good girl."

Aww, hear what she called me? I don't mean to brag or nothing, but my wife thinks I'm a good girl.

She gave me one of those quick pecks and said, "I'll make breakfast."

She was gone in a flash to go make breakfast, which is when I said, "Damn right you will" very quietly.

I don't know the name of her game, but I can say I didn't especially care for parts of it because as soon as breakfast was over and she had cleaned up (she volunteered to clean up, which is when I left the room and said, "Damn right you will.") she said, "Let's go," and took me by the wrist.

"Where?" You might think I'm paranoid, but there are some days when I don't trust her so much and wish I knew what was going to happen next. I mean, yes, I'm always three steps ahead of her, but sometimes that means I don't know what the first and second steps are. Really.

"To the potty, silly."

"Ourgh!"

"Is it that hard to hold it?"

"Marrry!" *Whisk* is the sound my pullup made as it reached my ankles. Her pullup. Hers. I ... dammit.

"Can you try to go for me," she asked with all the faux earnestness she can muster (which is a lot)

"Why am I naked again," I asked with my arms folded across my chest.

"Because big girls pee in the potty and not their pants, silly, but you have to sit down first."

"Stop smiling."

"Stop standing." *Well, touché?*

And then I was sitting. We should invest in heated toilet seats.

"Mary," I said and started to stand up and then these hands were on my shoulders preventing me – me! an agent of my own fate! – from standing.

"Five minutes."

I closed my eyes to gather my patience and said, "Fine. Can I get some privacy, please?"

"Of course not."

"Thank – what!?! Marrry! Get out," I didn't whine. No whining. I don't even know why people keep bringing up whining when I don't even do that ever. Really.

Mary knows when she's crossed a line. She knows when she's pushed me too far. That's why when I ordered her out of the bathroom, she sat down on the edge of the tub. *Dammit.*

"Are we really going to sit here for five minutes," I asked. Not many people can sit on the toilet because they were told to and maintain a regal level of dignity, but I can. Really. (Really? Please? Meh, really.)

"Well, if you tinkle before then, you can go back to playing after we clean your princess parts and wash our hands."

"What is even happening right now?" *WHAT DOES IT ALL MEAN!?!* Not that I ever stood under the night sky and shouted that, except when watching *Lost*. Real fuck it.

"You tinkle in the potty and …"

"You're giving me a headache."

"I'll rub your shoulders for you when the time is up."

"I'm not talking to you anymore." *La dee da, not talking to Mary. Not even looking at her. Staring off into space. My, what an interesting ceiling we have. LA DEE FRIGGIN' DA!*

"Guess you don't have to go," Mary I'm–so–clever said after five minutes. She actually set the timer on her phone. Like she's funny or something. She's not, ya know. I mean, she often is, but in the moment, not. N–O–T. "Let's get you dressed. Up."

"Does that mean I can have pants?"

"You're talking to me again," she asked as she pulled her pullup back into place over my parts. Who does she think she is? The building inspector? I say what goes over my plumbing. Me, and no one else. Except Mary. Dammit…

"No, I'm not talking to you again …. So is that a yes on the pants?"

"Nope. Snug as a bug in a pullup." See? She's not funny. She just tells corny dad jokes designed to afflict me. "Remember to come get me if you need to go."

I spent the next half hour googling bathroom use denial and adult potty training fetishes not being exactly sure which, if either, she was up to. She's nothing if not full of surprises and only too happy to explore new and exciting (for her, exclusively … mostly … some of the times … rarely) ways to tickle our erotic humiliation bones. My brain said *yellow light*, and my gut said *let's see where this goes* and my brain said to my gut *you always say that*, which is when I said, "You both have terrible instincts and suck in different ways. Equally, but in different ways."

Not that time seems to mean much anymore, but I looked at the time and wondered how it could be that twenty minutes could last a whole ten hours. Which is when my brain said *you have to pee*. And my gut said, *just go to the bathroom*. And my brain said, *that is so like you – first, you say let's wait and see, and then your instinct is to do exactly the thing that gets her butt spanked twice a week in a* good *week*. And my butt chimed in with, *yeah, ya jerk*.

I have to let my brain win some of these fights, if only to give my butt a chance to heal, so I went to Mary (because I'm good girl and one of the all–time great rule followers – really! please believe me!) and said, "I have to pee. What now?" Which I said because we all know she had some notion of what she wanted me to do next.

"Already?"

"Yep. So …" And I hinted toward the bathroom.

"But you just tried."

"I didn't have to go then, so could we …"

"Mmmm nah."

"'Nah'?" What the fuck is 'nah'? "What is 'nah'?"

"I just settled in to read the news."

"So do it in the bathroom!"

"Nah."

"Marrry!"

"O, just sit and snuggle with me."

Mixed signals! Unclear directions! Inadequate instructions! Terms not in common usage! Exhibit not in evidence! *GRRRRR!*

"What game are we even playing?!?"

"Same one we always play, sweetie. Sit." So it was a game of Torment Daphne after all. I should've known. All the signs were there.

"Buh – fine! But I'm gonna pout." I at least warn her before I do stuff like pout (occasionally). It's called courtesy. I'm the most courteous person, like Jeeves and Miss Manners had acrobatic courtesy sex and created a courtesy love child.

"I know. You're being a very good girl, by the way," she congratulated me without looking up from her phone to see what was one of the best angry–pouting faces I've ever made, and I've made at least, like, two. It could be more, but it's also not because I don't pout. That's just not me. Really.

But as to my being a good girl in that moment? "Urgh! I know and it sucks." Really – o no, like for realzies really.

There I sat, as useful as a lump on a log while Mary read on her phone and I did some conspicuous pouting–as–protest. This little monarchy of hers desperately needs a parliament. Something bicameral. And I should be one of the cameras (camere, technically). She read me the occasional headline, and I read the news plenty. I read the news so much sometimes she tells me I'm not allowed to read anymore news because it makes me anxious. I miss the boring decade from the first third of my life.

"Alright, let's go," she said all sunny like I'm supposed to be excited about this game. *AND WHAT ARE WE EVEN PLAYING!?!*

"Ugh. Fine." I followed her back to the bathroom.

"Alright," she said, "down those … aww, it's okay to have accidents. I guess it's my fault for not taking you to the potty sooner."

"Suhbuhdunuh higeruh hairen fruhtotter! (Sound of a bee swarm) and (steam escaping) and (alley cats fighting) and I'll sue! (Angry bear roars)! Defamation of character! (Bostonians shouting at a tourist in a roundabout.) Abuse of authority! (Gasoline catching fire) False advertising, bad rule making and kernoffler, Mary!" O, and there was a lot of fist clenching and stomping, too. Me, specifically, I did the fist clenching and stomping and turning red and giving out dirty looks like candy on a pre–covid Halloween.

Mary, instead of listening to the charges leveled against her, was going, "Hahahaha!"

"Stop laughing at me! (sniff)"

"Aww, c'mere. Let me make it all better." For the record, I only accepted her hug because I like her and her hugs a lot. Also, I only let her put her hand on the pullup because she didn't ask permission and I'm a good girl, dammit! (Dammit.) "You soaked this pullup. You couldn't wait another thirty minutes?"

"But you didn't say I had to wait another thirty minutes. You just said no," I didn't whine. "And the rule about the pullups and you … (huff)."

"Poor, sweet thing. Have you had enough trying for today?"

As in trying to play at whatever game she was playing? "Yes (sniff)"

"Alright, let's go change you back into one of your big girl diapers. I know you tried your hardest."

"So I'm not in trouble?" Not that it would be like Mary to invent a game I can't possibly win and spank me for losing. She'd nevvvver do that – really. (And that, folks, was my first – ever – sarcastic 'really.' Really).

"No, sweetie. You did a very good job. Besides, I don't spank for potty accidents because that would just be cruel." Which is when she winked at me, which is when my bottom lip started quivering because she pushed all my buttons. Like I said, she knows right where the edge is and not often but sometimes takes me right up to it. It's one thing to spank a person to tears. It's another thing to humiliate a person to tears. Right at the edge. She chuckled at my quivering lip and cooed, "Awww. Maybe you didn't get enough sleep. Do you wanna go back to bed for a while?"

"Mhmm." Remember an hour and a half prior when I didn't wanna get outta bed? Me too.

"Okay. Let's go get one your fluffy cloth diapers on." I would've protested, but I was kinda out of all the words by that point.

"Will you lay down with me?" Except those words.

"Yep, and I'll hold you real tight and stroke your cheek until you fall asleep."

"Can we have sex later?" Also, those words, but I was asking for my friend.

Chapter 8: Mary Gets Floopy and I Get a Quickie

"Where's my little critter?"

Her what now?

"Where's my little critter?"

"Um, are you referring to me," I asked from the living room as she came in sight around the corner. She had that derpy look she sometimes gets at the end of ten–hour workdays after having several ten–hour workdays in a row. Sure, if you work on your feet, you're physically tired after ten hours, and she gets physically tired (sitting for ten hours is seriously hard on the body) but she's a knowledge economy worker, according to the intelligentsia who name these things, and after ten hours three days in a row, she gets goofy.

I'm allowed to call it goofy to her face, just FYI. I called her derpy once and she made me take it back in a way that was only mostly fun.

"Yep," she said and plopped down next to me. She put her hands on my cheeks and pulled me in and started kissing me all over my face and just loving on me. As if! I mean, geez, summon some dignity why don'tcha. Really.

"Mary ch Mary – heehee – Mary – stop! You're embarrassing me on front of my friends."

"There's no one here but us, silly."

"Who you calling silly?" I was not being silly. I was being quirky. She was being silly. And derpy.

"You, silly!" Touché.

"Are you done with work now?"

"Mhmm. For eleven whole hours. What are we gonna do?" Yeah, I don't miss work anymore. I miss interacting with people. It was nice to walk into a room and know with a reasonable degree of certainty I'd walk out with my butt in the same condition as when I went in (though this one time when I was working at band camp...).

But working all day, barely having any me time, and then doing it again? What a stupid idea. I mean, first they pave over nature so you can't live a hunter–gatherer lifestyle even if you want to, then they stop teaching which berries are poisonous in the schools and how to wear a moose. Which would work because Mary says I look good in anything, but sometimes I wonder how much to trust her word when she gets all derpy. Glad I never get derpy. Just because she makes me go all a–flutter until I go *ha!* and make my smitten–kitten face doesn't mean I ever get derpy. Really.

"I'll make dinner while you go change into something more comfortable," I offered. Mary looked down at herself.

"I'm wearing sweatpants and a tee shirt," she said because she finally joined the rest of the world in giving up on clothes with buttons.

"Well," I suggested, "you could put on a tee shirt too grubby to leave the house in."

"I'd rather sit here with you and wait for dinner to get here."

"What did you order?"

"Food. Who cares anymore? I'm tired of figuring out dinner every night."

"Ahem." I've been doing ninety (thousand) percent of the cooking. We cook together some nights, especially weekends, but since she's buying the food and doing all the income earning, I'm doing the cooking. Fair is fair. Plus it gives me something to do. Plus I can get away with (less) healthier meals when she's not cooking.

"I mean," she backpedaled, "I'm tired of letting you do all the work."

"Nice save. You're being goofy."

"I'm out of working brain parts."

"You're talking like me," I said.

"You're a bad influence. And pizza. I ordered pizza."

"Hmm," I said, "I hope it has a garlic–butter crust so you won't wanna kiss me tonight."

"Is that your way of asking for a quickie before it gets here?" See, she must have some working brain parts. The parts that live in the gutter, but still.

"You're the one who came in here all floopy and kissing me everywhere. You're making me think you have some unrequited thing for me. It's sad really. How sad for you."

Hoo boy! She requited the stuffing outta me. And then promptly fell asleep. I had pizza and stroked her hair while she slept. Does that mean I'm a switch now? Probably not. It was a good day.

Chapter 9: And Those Were My Favorite Panties

It was getting to be a long day. Somewhere between working and not working there must be some happy place where the days don't get ridiculously long. Maybe it's because the pandemic means I can't go anywhere. I like to at least imagine that if I could go places and see people and do things that this state of semi–retirement would be more fun.

So what did I do? I made breakfast for us, then I watched the *Today Show*, doom scrolled through social media, and tried to find a new book to read that wasn't erotica. I used to read all the time. I don't know what gives now, but lately I just can't seem to get into a good book. I blame social media and the internet. I think they killed my attention span. MTV killed the radio star; the internet killed the attention span.

Then I made lunch for us and decided after, when Mary was back in her office and couldn't say no, to make no–bake cookies. But I make them with protein powder and they're high in fiber, so at least they have some nutritional goodness. Ya know those crisper containers that keep vegetables fresh in the fridge for longer? I put the cookies in there. Not to hide them but because it's big and I made lots of cookies.

I went to take Mary a cookie and ask for assistance with a thing and found her office door closed. Granted, it took a couple spankings, but I remembered I'm not supposed to go in or knock if she has the door closed. I didn't want the cookie to spoil, so I ate it just in case she was going to be in her office for fourteen days (waste not, want not and all that and stuff) and texted her.

She texted me back, "I'm on calls for the next couple hours. You can change it."

Well, not that I don't know how, but I still haven't done that, and I don't want to. They really are Mary's diapers, and why should I have to put something on me that I don't even want? That'd be like her telling me to spank myself, and I haven't done that since I was single and lonely. (Because sometimes back then, I needed a reminder to behave myself, but more specifically I needed a reminder that a hot, smarting bottom made my woohoo parts go *woohoo*!)

I went up to our bedroom and just took the diaper off, did some hygiene stuff to freshen up, and put on panties. I spent a little time looking in the mirror, too. I had a strange impulse that morning to look like I actually had somewhere to go, and not just somewhere, but somewhere nice. I put on a dress and did my hair (sort of – I don't know what to do with my long hair and I wanna get a haircut) and even a little makeup and earrings. I was looking very pretty, if I say so myself (and I did, so there).

And since I was looking so pretty, I decided to do what all pretty girls do and play *Assassin's Creed*. Is it me, or are the cut scenes a total waste of time?

"Daphne Ann," Mary said as she startled me out of my virtual parkour.

"Hi. Done with work?"

"What game are you playing? You just eviscerated that person!"

"Ha! Yeah." Good times.

"We need to get you some nice games for little girls."

Which I countered with a dirty look and, "But this *is* a nice game, and I'm *not* a little girl."

"Just because you put on a little blush doesn't mean you're a big girl. For one thing, big girls know how to sit when they're in a dress." Okay, for the record, I was in video game stance. It's not pretty, but it is effective. "Hold still and let me check your undies."

She can really move fast when it involves my nethers. She's like the Green Lantern (what was his superpower?) or the Flash or Usain Bolt. But I'm faster (when there's a coffee table between us) and moved out of video game stance into crossing my legs stance. "No," I said.

"Excuse me?"

"You don't need to check anything. I'm fine."

"Someone's in a mood."

"Yeah, you." With her teasing and video game criticism and I did a really good job putting on my makeup, which is a ridiculous thing for someone my age to be proud of, but I hadn't done it in I don't even know how long, and I did good. What did she do all day except keep the internet on? Like that's a public service or something.

"What's gotten into you," she asked as she sat down next to me and pushed me (she pushed me! well, more of a nudge, but she pushed me!) just enough so she could get a hand under my butt. "Daphne Ann Taylor, where is your diaper, young lady?"

O my god, she was soooo in a mood if she went and trotted out all three of my names, and I didn't even do anything. Granted, I told her no, which is against the rules, but she was being snippy with me before I even said that. And yeah, we were both snippy, but she started it (you don't think she knows I ate her cookie, do you?).

"I took it off. You said I could."

"I said you could change it. I did not say you could change out of it."

"Well, how was I supposed to know that?"

"O, don't even try that. That's why you didn't want me to check."

"I didn't want you to check because there's nothing to check!" There's no condition down there that was in need of checking! At the time.

"So you're really going to sit there and tell me that when you went upstairs to change you didn't even spend one second considering whether to put a new one on? And don't dig a deeper hole for yourself and fib."

"That just means you've already decided what the truth is," I pointed out. I'm good at pointing stuff out. Such as, *o look, a squirrel and a five–foot–ten lezdom who's being really unfair.*

"So what is the truth?"

"(Sound of a gentle breeze through a canyon)"

"That's what I thought. Let's go."

"Buh – urgh!" *SWAT.* "Eep!"

"That wouldn't have hurt if you had your diaper on."

"It wouldn't hurt if you had learned to keep your hands to yourself!" We learn that in pre–school where I come from, and it's a very good guide to life and she should *SMACK!* "Ow! Marrry! Slow down at least." She has longer legs than me. I'm a tiny little woman!

"You can scurry just fine when you want to." And yeah, but that, like, wasn't a convenient fact for me right then. Really.

She took me right to the bedroom and sat me down on the edge of the bed, folded her arms, cocked her head, and asked, "Are you having a mini rebellion today?" To which I rolled my eyes. I'm allowed to roll my eyes. They're mine, and they're in my head, so I can do what I want with them. Which is when she shook her head and went, "Tsk tsk tsk," and sighed. "I see the problem now. I can't believe this is still a thing. Stand up."

"There's no problem," I said as I stood up.

"O yes there is, too. You're wearing big girl clothes, and you think that makes you a big girl." She lifted my dress above my waist. "Black satin," she said and put her hand right on my black satin panties. "Satin is hard to wash, Daphne. That's why it's for big girls and not pee pants girls."

Now, you may hear from misinformed third parties that my reaction to that comment was unrefined, perhaps even a tantrum, or that it went something like, "(Foot stomp) You are (sound of hail falling on a tin roof) and (twenty–car pileup) and (lightning striking a power station) and just so (cattle stampede) and being unfair (red–faced, fist–clenched adult out of breath), Mary!"

But I don't know where these third parties get their information, because what I said was, "How true. Good thing I'm an adult and not a pee pants." Really.

It was Mary who was out of control with her whole recrossing her arms and looking at me with her you've–got–to–be–kidding-me face and her we've–had–this–conversation–before tone when she said, "Turn around."

"Eurgh!" But I did turn around, and you know why? Because I'm a good girl (and stomping your foot doesn't make you not a good girl. It makes you a good girl who stomps her feet, but only because of all the injustice she's subject to).

"It's nice that you wanna be a grown up and wear pretty dresses," she soliloquized as she unzipped my dress, "and put on makeup. I'm sure it makes you feel very mature. Step out." And then I was in just my panties and my bra. Unless you count the sour expression I was wearing. "Let's hang this up," Mary said. So she did. It was my turn to fold my arms across my chest and glare. So I did.

She put her arm around my shoulder and guided me to my dresser. "And jewelry, too. Tsk tsk."

"Stop tsking me!"

"Hold still for me, little girl." Dammit! "Let's just get these out and put them back where they're safe." And she took my earrings out and put them away.

Ya know, I actually really like it when Mary undresses me, but not when she's being mean. AND I AM TOO A BIG GIRL, DAMMIT! I can wear what I want when I want (unless Mary says otherwise … dammit).

"And let's go get that makeup off your face." So we went to the bathroom and I endured her taking the blush off my cheeks (which under the circumstances didn't make them any less red) and the lipstick, too. "There." She turned me to face the mirror. "You don't need to hide that pretty skin at your age." Okay, that was maybe sincere and a nice compliment, but still.

"And this little bralette. Arms up." And she took off my bra(lette) and tossed it in the hamper. I was in just my panties, which don't cover much, which is fine in summer, but our bedroom is chilly in winter and there were goosebumps (which does not make me a silly goose – really!). "Let's go." She took me back into the bedroom and sat down on the chair. "Over my knee. Time for your spanking."

"Emmmmmurgh!" I growled (didn't wine – I don't do that, as I've said, and if I ever find the person who started that rumor, I'm gonna sic Mary on them) and I put myself over her lap. Sometimes being a good girl is seriously disadvantageous.

"When I put you in a diaper and let you change it, that means put another one on, doesn't it?"

"But you didn't say that. How am I supposed to know what you want with this stuff when you won't tell me?" And the thing is, that was about forty percent a good faith question. As to the other sixty percent, well, never you mind. Don't be nosy.

"But you did know what I meant, didn't you? … We'll stay just like this until you answer me."

"Yes."

"Yes, you did. And you also told me no downstairs. Are you allowed to tell me no when I tell you to do something?"

"No."

"And why not?"

"Because you're in charge."

"That's right. I'm in charge, and little girls are not in charge. What happens when you don't follow the rules like I've taught you to?"

"I get in trouble."

"And what happens then? Do you get grounded?"

"No."

"Do you get your allowance taken away?"

"No." Probably helps that I'm not on an allowance.

"Then when happens?"

"I get spanked."

"That's right. I spank your bottom, just like a naughty little girl."

"I'm not a little girl!"

She took the waistband of my panties and snapped them, which made me eep just a little. "Are these still making you feel like a big girl? Because from where I'm sitting, it just looks like you borrowed your big sister's panties without permission."

Okay, so in other contexts, that little scenario would make me cum in my big sister's panties. In the actual thing happening at the moment, it did not. It so did not. "(Sniff). Why are you being so mean to me today?"

"Honey, I discipline you and give you consequences because I love you and want you to learn right from wrong. If you had followed the rules, you wouldn't be over my knee about to get your bottom spanked, would you?"

"No (sniff)."

"And I'm sorry I have to give you this spanking. I'd much rather play with you after work than have to spank."

O. My. God. She is such a fibber. One of these days I'm going to put soap in her toothbrush just so she can learn a lesson the same way she's tried to teach me to not fib.

She squeezed my butt. "This could've been avoided if you had just followed directions. You could still be wearing your pretty dress and not be over my knee. You think about that while I'm giving you your spanking." I was within an inch of my life of just telling her to shut up already, and another inch of dissolving into sobs, and I don't even know why.

SMACK SMACK.

"I'm sorry I had to do that."

"Emmmmmm buhoohoohoo (snort-sob)." She didn't even do it right! I've gotten two spanks for crossing the living room while in possession of a butt! *Waaaaah!*

"Shh shh. I know that hurt. And you were very brave." And she was rubbing my shoulders and stroking my back. "Can you sit up for me?"

Yes, but tearfully, is how to translate my, "Mmmm (sniff)."

"There there," She cooed and and stroked my hair.

"I don't even know what you're doing," I very honestly whined (but seriously, who starts these rumors about me whining?). She was being mean and somehow nice and it was confusing.

"Silly girl, I gave you a spanking."

"No you didn't."

"I gave you a little girl spanking because you're my little girl. Now let's get you redressed, okay?"

"Mhmm." She sorta pivoted so I was sitting in the chair and she was standing. I wouldn't call it a ninja move, but there was athleticism there.

Instead of going to my dresser, she went into the closet and – big surprise – emerged with diapers and a long–sleeve onesie I was hoping she was saving for never.

"I know a little girl who probably has cold toes, am I right," she asked. She got some of my fuzzy socks to add to the ensemble. "Let's get these on you first. Gimme one of these feetsies." I did, and she didn't exactly tickle it, but she did run a fingertip down the sole of my foot, and it made me curl my toes. I remember from way back in school they taught us that's a reflex they test for in newborns. I remember from way back when that I like it when she rubs my feet and does gentle tickles. I don't like the furious tickling, but I like the gentle kind.

When I had my socks on, she ordered, "Put 'em up," and she pulled the onesie over my head. "Where'd Daphne go!?! Dere she is!"

"Hehe. Mary, stop."

"No."

"Grr!"

"Come on, let's get you back in a diaper where you belong."

Excuse me? "Marrry, I do not." But I did get on the bed and lay back. I wish she wouldn't say stuff like that.

She bent down over me right next to my ear and whispered, "You do if I say you do," and gave my earlobe a nibble. "But," she said with her I'm–springing–a–surprise–you'll–hate–and–I'll–love tone (her eyes always get bright and shiny when she does that), "I understand that sometimes you wanna feel grown up, so you can keep the undies on."

"Good," I said and started to sit up.

"Where are you going," she said with a hand on my chest stopping me part way.

We didn't use words for what passed between us next. We did the whole thing with facial expressions and eyebrow gestures.

You can't be serious.

O yes I am.

No.

Yes.

Marrrry!

This is happening.

"No. Mary, no."

"Lay back down."

"No, I'm not gonna." She could never spank me long enough or hard enough to make me pee in my panties.

"Daphne," she said with one of those meaningful looks of hers, "do as you're told."

Urgh!!!!! Unfair! It's hard being a good girl, and it's even harder being a submissive good girl. Telling me to do as I'm told may as well be threatening me with kryptonite and snakes. It got me all started with the trembling lip and hyperventilating. "Please," I moaned.

"It'll be okay," she reassured me. "Just lay back and let me take care of it." I did and put my arms over my eyes and had my own private pity party (with tears as a party favor). "Shh shh shh. Everything will be fine. Lift your bottom for me."

I did, and she got a cloth diaper under me. I could tell she had a stuffer in it, too (I'm wishing I'd never learned the lingo).

"Open your legs for me ... good girl. You're being a very good girl."

O, like I didn't know how good I was being. I was being great. She folded the diaper over me and tugged to get it snug and velcroed me in.

"Lift again." And in a repeat of the process, she got plastic panties on me, the kind with the snaps. I like those a little more than the other, but that still leaves them in the despised category.

My pity party skipped over rave and went straight to post–rave–drunk–girl–panic–attack. It's more fun when you're drunk, and it's not even fun at all when you're drunk. Thankfully, Mary knows the signs and laid down next to me, pulling me over so I could cry into her shirt.

"You're okay," she whispered.

Long–term, sure. Right then? Nope. Nopety–nope–nope–nope.

She made a snarky comment about my game, implied I wasn't mature enough for makeup and jewelry, made me take off my dress, talked down to me like I'm a little girl, (viciously) spanked me, and put a diaper on over my panties. She made me wet my panties! (Eventually, not yet then). And I liked those panties! And satin is hard to wash! Really!!! She said so! Grrr!!!

"Umsudatu," I said.

"What's that, baby?"

"I'm so mad at you," I sob–said.

"Aww. That's okay. You go right ahead and be mad because I love you forever and always no matter what."

O. my. God. Was it that she didn't know or didn't care that saying that would make me bawl? You don't say stuff like that to me when I'm already a mess unless you're just looking to turn me into an emotional dumpster fire. Which, yeah, sometimes is helpful with the purging of the feelings, but there's a time and a place and "Waaaaaaaaaah haaaah haaaah!" I may have even gone, "Boohoohoohoo!"

"I know. Get it all out. It's my fault ..." O, goodie, something we agree on. "... for letting you get dressed like a big girl. I think those clothes just made you forget your place." Dammit.

Nope nope nope nope nope – fuck it. "Idunhafapace!"

"Of course you do, sweetheart. Your place is right next to my side as my submissive little girl."

"Umntaittlegrl!"

"But you're my little girl." And then she kissed me on the temple. And then she did it again. And then she kissed me on my cheek and my neck. Such effrontery from a peasant.

"Iwuntduit."

"What won't you do, Daffodil."

"Put a diaper on myself. I won't do it. I don't even like them. You hafta do it if you want me to wear 'em."

"Okay."

"And you tease too much sometimes."

"I do?"

"I got all dressed up today, and you made it a thing."

"I'm sorry. Did I hurt your feelings?"

"A little. (sniff)." O. My. God. I. Am. Pathetic. Sometimes, anyway.

"Then I'm very sorry. Can I tell you something that might make it up you?"

"Yes." She'd better if she knew what was good for me (which she usually does).

"You were very pretty in your dress."

"Thank you. I did a good job on my makeup, too."

"Yes, you did."

"Yes, I did."

"My pretty girl."

But on another urgent matter in need of resolution before things were done that could not be undone, "Do I really gotta pee my panties?"

"Mhmm. Sorry, Daff, but actions have consequences."

"Then what's your consequence for teasing me?"

"I'll make you dinner and let you hang on me all evening."

"And who said I wanna hang on you," I pouted as I burrowed back into her chest.

"Such a snuggly little girl."

"And?"

"A good girl."

"A very good girl."

"My very good girl. Let's go wash my pretty, good girl's face."

"Do the buttons first. And can I have pants?"

"Nope, but we can sit in front of the fire. How's that," she asked as she snapped the onesie shut.

"It's terrible."

"Such a silly good girl. I love you muchly."

"I love you muchly more."

Chapter 10: On Listening the First Time

I don't think you all realize what kind of person Mary is. You all think she's great, but I've been trying to tell you just how evil she is: she's the kind of evil that would strangle a baby panda.

And I say that because she said the meanest thing she's ever said to me. Or not to me, but about me and with me sitting right there. And it was so mean it's evil! I won't even tell you what she said because some of the evil would rub off on me and I'd have to break quarantine and go to church and apologize to god!

So I'll just tell you what I said in response to her evilness.

"I DID NOT HAVE STINKY PANTS!"

Deep breath, wait for my heart to slow down, kiss a crucifix, wash the bad feelings away, and rewind.

I put on five pounds with my Christmas–slash–pandemic–induced–stress baking. Which, yeah, isn't a lot, but it shows on me. I didn't notice it at first, though I suspect Mary did and was just being nice not saying anything. But when I put my yoga pants on and looked in the mirror, I think my exact words were, "What the fuck is that?"

"What," Mary asked.

"This! Is it – it wasn't there last week."

Mary had her I'm–not–so–sure–about–that look on her face and said, "I'm not so sure about that." See?

She waltzed right up to me and squeezed it. Or tried to because it disappeared when she did, but it popped right back out. "Someone's got a little jelly roll."

"Eeeeegyuh! No more cookies and peanut butter."

"Gee, who said that twenty baking sessions ago?"

"It's sad how you live in the past, Mary." Sad, but understandable. It's her coping mechanism. Some of us bravely live in the present, ready to take whatever life can throw at us with a steely resolve like me, and some of us can't, like Mary. Really. (What? Really.)

"Can I offer a suggestion," Mary asked.

"Only if it's nice."

"You could use that athleisure outfit of yours to do something athletic to go along with all the leisure."

Harsh. So harsh. But also right, which makes it even more harsh. Though I wouldn't call all of my downtime leisure. I'd call it unstructured play, which is important for developing creativity and imagination. Also, I am a lady of leisure, which is what I now call myself instead of unemployed or housewife or stay–at–home–partner or homemaker. Though I am all of those things except for the first one.

So downstairs to our basement gym I went, and I removed the various pieces of laundry hanging on the exercycle I bought at some point in my misspent past. As a stationary bike, not the best brand, but as a thing to hang delicates and shrinkables on to dry, also not the best brand. I dusted off the bluetooth speaker that amazingly still works after not having been used in let's-not-quantify-my-laziness (but really, leisure – I'm very intrepid), and I got to work.

Now, you don't lose weight by exercise. You lose it by dieting. But the exercise helps, and not having been to the gym, walked up the stairs in a parking garage, or done much of anything besides a leisurely walk in almost a year, you might say I was still slim on the outside, the five pounds my yoga pants revealed as a little flub of flubber notwithstanding, but I had gotten very fat on the inside. I exercycled as far as my almost atrophied legs and lungs could take me in a half hour, or almost a half hour, when Mary came to the top of the stairs and walked down to congratulate me on my first step toward better health.

She went, "Turn it down!" I guess the congratulatory part was silent.

"What?"

"TURN IT DOWN!" And she turned off my speaker. "I'm glad you're doing this and hope you do it tomorrow, but you can't blast your music while I'm working. The noise goes right up the vent to the guest room. Here," she said and held out the headphones I bought (for more than the agreed upon spending limit) but that Mary let me keep (after paddling me with the school paddle). I'm still walking funny from that one. Or the seven or eight since. Who's to say? I'm not a doctor.

"Sorry ... and thank you."

She made her Daphne–is–yummy face and put her hand rather suggestively on my arm. "You're a little sweat ball."

"Am not! I'm just glistening." We've been over this. I glisten. Pigs sweat. Woodland creatures such as myself glisten.

"Can't remember the last time I saw you so sweaty outside the sheets."

"It's not sweat. It's … whatever substance makes us glisten."

"Us?"

"Me and other sylphs and water nymphs."

"Ha! Don't strain yourself."

"I won't. I'm an experienced athlete … who's hasn't athleted in a while."

Mary went back to her work, and I went back to mine, which is when I remembered how much harder it is after you stop for a few minutes but how easy it is to take a break.

I have the willpower of a golden retriever, the impulse control of a golden retriever, and the appetites of an *intact* golden retriever. I can sense you shaking your heads what with my normally stoic and even ascetic approach to life, but it's true. Sometimes I just can't help myself when it comes to whatever endorphin- or oxytocin-inducing thing I set my mind on, and no sooner do I satisfy that desire than my mind finds another pleasure-inducing thing to want. I find the best way to deal with this is to remove the temptation entirely. Of course, many of those appetites and accompanying temptations are called Mary, but at least I can throw out the junk food.

You might be wondering if Mary would be mad at me for throwing out the junk food, and the answer is no because she's one of those freaks who doesn't crave it like it's the best thing since me. Which is totally unfair. I mean, I was addicted to Diet Coke from the age of friggin' four, but at least I managed to stay my svelte little self growing up in the land of BBQ Jalapeño Ranch Everything. The Wisconsin climate and diet aren't friendly for us naturally cold, hungry, and addictive types.

With nothing else to do, I went back down to the basement after lunch for some strength training. We have bands and kettlebells and some dumbbells acquired here and there from our various dalliances with fitness trends. I hoisted and carried and lifted and put down and pronated and supinated and extended and contracted and … stuff. That's when I realized two things. Firstly, I should make an actual plan for my exercising. Second and more immediately, I was in trouble.

How did I know I was in trouble? I saw Mary's irritable feet coming down the stairs. Only Mary could manage to have irritable feet. The normal folk out there like you and me just have irritable expressions, but even in her work slippers (I invented that category of footwear just for her), she can have irritable feet.

"Daphne, I told you to use your headphones."

Obviously, I was using my headphones because … dammit.

"I must've left them upstairs when I took a break. Sorry." Also, breaks can be three hours long. I decided. On this, I am the decider. Really.

"A little late for sorry. I had to get off a conference call because your dance party is coming through the vent." Which is when I saw …

"Mary, not the … urgh."

"Yep, this might make you remember when I tell you something. Grab your knees."

I hate the school paddle! It's so … big. And I'm not! Why couldn't I gain all five pounds in my ass? *Stupid weight gain and stupid paddle and stupid HVAC system.* I wasn't even playing my music that loud.

"Can't we talk about this," I asked in what apparently came across as a rhetorical question because Mary took me by my shoulder, turned me, and bent me forward.

"We can talk about it tonight after your paddling and when I'm done with work."

WHAP! "Eep!" WHAP!!! "Yow!!" Sniffle.

"Headphones," she said and kissed me. "I have to get back on that call."

And she kissed me again. That's the second time those headphones got me paddled by Assistant Vice Principal for Buzzkilling Mary. And yes, it's the headphones' fault, not mine. Really.

And did I mention OW! I can't believe it's legal to do that to anyone but a consenting adult because OW!!! My butt hurt, and just above that and around the corner was a little ball of tummy dread because often, but not always but often and frequently, if Mary gets out the school paddle I get another spanking the same day. You may not have noticed, but I've kinda been not getting spanked as frequently as I was before. Like maybe just once (and a half) a week (on average) as compared to twice (and a third time), and I was kinda enjoying not spending so much time in the corner. I was getting playful good girl spankings to make up for it, which is key to a happy Daffy. And approximate rhyme is not a spanking offense. Really. Besides, *happy Daffy* assonates. Go look it up.

I finished my workout and spent some time examining my butt (marks with just two swats! that thing should be added to the list of weapons of ass destruction), and checking out my figure. Not because I'm vain but because good health demands it. And also vanity.

I went downstairs to the kitchen for a post–workout snack of healthy fruits and nuts, and there was Mary. "I'm sorry about the music," I said.

"Everything travels right up the vent, and why do you play it so loud anyway?"

"I was feeling the burn?"

"And how does your bottom feel now?"

"It burns." Har har. She pulled a chair out from the kitchen table and turned it so it was facing the room. "Aww, c'mon. You already spanked me. I won't do it again."

"What's the rule about getting spanked at school?"

"What are you even talking about?"

"Did you get your bottom paddled today?"

"Mary …

"Daphne Ann, I asked you a question, little girl."

"Yes." And I am NOT a little girl! Dammit!

"And what kind of paddle was it?"

"School paddle."

"So you must've gotten your bottom paddled at school, and what's the rule about getting spanked away from home?"

"But that's only if I get spanked by someone else,"

"And during business hours, I'm Senior Vice President Taylor, who had to drop off a meeting to go downstairs and discipline you."

"But that's not fair!" I didn't stomp my foot. It was more like half a stomp. Just my heel came up, so that doesn't count.

"Who whines about fairness?"

"Marrrry!" And who even whines? Not me. It's those other people. They're the whiners.

"Do I need to make you say it?"

Ooo, this one time she made me say something by … anyhoo. "Little kids and hypocritical politicians whine about fairness," I grumbled.

"And have you been elected or appointed to an office I don't know about?"

Well, I am Empress, but that's a secret, so, "No."

"Then I guess we know what you are. Come here to me." I got within arm's length before she took my wrist and pulled me over her lap.

"But it still hurts from the paddling!"

"I imagine it does." SMACK! Mary and her stupid imagination. SMACK! SMACK! SMACK! And so forth. I mean, you must know the routine by now. Me over Mary's getting spanked like a (little) giantess who bestrides the world (or Mary's lap) stoically (grunting and verbalizing my growing discomfort) as I accept the injustice (though this time it was debatable) of the world as I take the sins of others (who are me) upon myself (butt).

"I said I was sorry."

"And I (spank) accept (spank) your apology (spank) but that (spank) doesn't (spank) mean (spank) you get (spank) out (spank) of (spank) your (spank) pun– (spank) ish– (spank) ment (spank)."

"Why are you making so big a deal out of this?"

"Because (spank) I shouldn't (spank) have to tell you (spank) things twice, but if I do (SPANK), then I guess (spank) you need to be (spank) spanked twice (spank spank spank)."

"Mary, that – ow! Okay – ow! I won't do it again. I'll list– ow! Fuck muffins."

"Excuse me, what did you say?"

"Fuck cupcakes? Teehee?" SPANK!!!! "Furple!" I exclaimed for some reason, I guess. I only have good reasons for the things I do and say. Really.

"Little girls do not swear during their spankings, and they don't get to keep their pants up, either."

"No, Mary, please? Not bare. It already – ouchie!"

Holy fuck, Daphne, did you just say ouchie, asked the mean girl voice in my head.

So what if I did, the sensitive girl shot back.

So this pandemic really is turning you into a little girl.

But it hurts!

It's a hand spanking!

So? Like you've ever been on the receiving end of Mary's hand.

Hello? We share a butt, remember?

You're a butt.

Said the little girl with her playground comeback.

Shut up!

"Owie!"

Aww, did the little girl get a spanking on her bare bottom from the big mean Mary?

She's not mean! She's just strict because I ("Oof!") *asked her to be.*

Let me guess – first you're gonna cry, and then you're gonna sit in her lap and cuddle?

Yes! So what? ... And shut up, ya big buttface.

"(Subsonic mouse cries)." SPANK! "Myeh."

What was that?

95

It was a high–pitched sob, now shut up already!

"Ehuh ehuh ehuh waaaaaah!"

She's still spanking you, if you thought crying was going to make her stop, which would at least be a good excuse for carrying on like a little girl.

Waaaaaaaah!

Yep, crying just like a little girl.

Am not! I'm just crying.

Now she's not spanking you, but you're still crying.

I know – (sniff).

"Shh shh shh," Mary cooed while rubbing my butt.

And we did cuddle, and she did wash my face and call me pretty, and she did hold up a paper towel and tell me to honk, etcetera, etcetera. I got a good summation lecture about listening the first time and being on my best behavior during business hours. Etcetera.

But then Mary had to go and be Mary and answer the phone after dinner. "Hey, Brenna."

"Hey. Just calling to see how you guys are doing."

"We want out," Mary said.

"Same. How's Daphne?"

"You can ask her yourself." And I'd have been happy to talk except Mary didn't just let me talk. She had to turn on the video which sent me scrambling for a blanket to pull up to my chin because I was dressed … for bed. Meaning naked, um, really. Naked, and wearing … something.

"Hi," I said.

"Hi. Are you feeling shy?"

"Um, I'm naked."

"She is not," Mary helpfully chimed in. My wife, my lover, my helpmeet, that's Mary, who's also a narc. "She's just shy because she's dressed for bed."

"It's only 7:30. What happened, Daffy? Did you get an early bedtime?"

"No," Mary said. "I just like her in her jammies. But she did get her bottom spanked today."

"Marrry!"

"Brenna knows all about little girls who need their bottom spanked, including yours."

"I'm not a little girl," I said as I absentmindedly chewed on the edge of the blanket. "Can I come live with you?"

"No, you may not, little girl," Mary said and kissed me on my temple. "I wanna keep you."

Not to change the subject, but Mary wants to keep me and she gives me temple kisses (though my whole body is a temple) which made me get this all over tingly, warm sensation.

And that sensation lasted right up until Mary said, "Besides, Brenna, she's an awful lot of work. When I put her over my knee, Little Miss Sass Bottom here had stinky pants."

"Muh," said I.

"No way," Brenna laughed.

"Buh," said me.

"Very stinky."

"She is such a little girl," said Brenna

Well, I am many things. I am an empress. I am a temple. I am someone who is going crazy in the pandemic times and gets in fights with herself in her own head while getting spanked. But – BUT! "I am not a little girl and I DID NOT HAVE STINKY PANTS!"

"It's okay," Brenna said. "You do what …."

"I was working out! I was sweaty! I didn't!"

"Maybe she does need that early bedtime," Brenna speculated because I don't know why. "She's getting herself all worked up over some stinky britches."

"Marrry, see what you did?"

"Yep. You wanna see her bedtime outfit," Mary asked.

"No," I declared. Not just any declaration but one of those infallible ones just us popes and empresses get to make. And I gripped the blanket, now pulled up to just under my nose, in case Mary tried to make me.

"But if you wanna live with her she's gonna need to know how to dress you properly."

"I can dress myself."

"But you told me just the other day that you don't wanna put your diapers on yourself."

"Marrrry!" Embarrassed, pleading puppy dogs were turned all the way up to eleven. They're one of the main weapons at the disposal of empresses (such as myself).

"Sorry," Brenna said, "I don't change stinky diapers."

"I didn't," I squeaked and turned toward Mary and buried my face in the space between her back and the couch. I was taught at a young age by a very kind child psychologist to take a break when needed to regather my patience and thoughts to deal with heightened anxiety and stress, and I needed such a moment and a private place to take it, and purely by happenstance, hiding behind Mary was (and frequently is) a good place to have a minute to myself. So let's not read any more into it than that.

The rest of their conversation was brief and muffled. Something about cooking? Anyway ...

"You can come out now," Mary said as she leaned just a little bit away from me.

"Why'd you tell her that," I asked.

"Because a little embarrassment is a good reminder to certain little girls to behave. And you know why else," she said with a lascivious grin.

Yes, yes I do know why else. "I'm not a little girl." Really!!! "My diaper is wet." Hers! Dammit ...

"Already? I just put it on you twenty minutes ago, and you pottied right before."

"It's not pee." (Sniff)

"You need a little help with that?"

"Yes please." (Sniff)

"Lie back back for me, baby."

"I'm not a baby."

"I think we'll start calling this is a number three."

"Ehhhehrm!"

"Such a grumpy girl."

"I'm not grumpy. I'm frustrated and impatient and my butt still hurts."

"Aww (crinkle) is your bottom all red and sore under your diapee (crinkle)?"

"Urr." With her hands (crinkle) pressing in (crinkle). "Yes."

"Wanna tell me what happened?"

"I got – hhh – my bare bottom – hhhh– spanked for diso – urgggggm – beying."

"And you had stinky pants when you got your spanking, didn't you?"

"Ffffffff no."

"Yes you did."

"Ffff mmmmm nnnno."

"Yes you did."

"Hhhh hh hh hhhhhh mm mm mm … … … …. …. …… (Sigh)." Welp, that was quick, mayhaps an indication of just how revved she had my little engine … which leave time for seconds and thirdsies before bed. Also, "No I didn't. …. Wanna turn?"

"Heehee. My little Daffodil. God bless whoever taught you about taking turns."

"Heeeheeee."

"It's one of the things that makes you such a good girl."

Oooo, my wife thinks I'm a good girl. And I am. Really. Heeheee.

Chapter 11: Since When Are We Into Ageplay?

It was months ago now that I finally accused Mary of being a big and started wondering where that came from and when it started, and she had done a very good job avoiding the subject. Good if not always subtle, "Like, Mary, how did you get interested in ageplay?"

And Mary's good but not subtle evasion was, "Over my knee."

"Why? I didn't do anything?" She didn't exactly give me a choice or a satisfactory explanation ("You're a red head." Ginger prejudice in my own house! Besides, I'm a day walker.)

I don't why she won't just talk about it. She said before it's because she thought ageplay goes so well with our domestic discipline and humiliation kinks, and I agree that it does, but that was more to do with her sudden interest in absorbent undergarments and not so much with the general ageplay. Or maybe her interest in absorbent undergarments wasn't so sudden, but if I can't get her to talk about her ageplay interest, I doubt she'll come clean on just how long ago her Daphne–in–diapers kink originated.

I turned to my unpublished journals from years past (tentatively titled *I Don't Wanna Be a Little Girl*, copyright, boilerplate, boilerplate, forthcoming in late 2022, maybe) to see if somewhere in our history there was a moment the ageplay thing started, because we've been together almost seven years and married for almost three, and the ageplay started before we got married, subtly for sure, but also I'm sure of that (don't question my sentence structure). I mean, she started calling me *little girl* not long after we became an item, but that's not the same as ageplay.

What I came up with was a scene we did at a play party put on by the same kink group we did that humiliation demonstration for, in The Before Times when we could do stuff like that. We'd been dating for a year, so we were past the point of Mary only spanking me in negotiated scenes but before I told her I wanted to go full lifestyle, and an acquaintance named Catherine wanted to arrange a group scene with some other spanking couples. Mary and me were quite happy to oblige. Sorta the point of play parties, and this party was a monthly thing in a big warehouse event space so we could do our thing and people could do whatever else elsewhere.

The scene Catherine wanted to do was a school principal scene. Right away that's kinda ageplay, but if we define ageplay as getting off on any woman in a cheerleader outfit then every person ever would qualify as an ageplayer, so it wasn't that. Nor did Catherine want to spank me or my fellow bottoms' bottoms. She wanted to sit back and, well, maybe it's better shown than told.

I was facing a wall along with four of my "friends." Well, we were friends or at least friendly, but in our scene, we were school friends. The five of us, three women and two boys, were caught skipping class and smoking reefer (did I mention Catherine was, like, sixty when we did this scene?), and our parents (tops and dommes) had been called to school to deal with us.

"I've given them demerits, detentions, kept them after, and even had the janitors put them to work, but nothing is getting through to them," Assistant Principal for Discipline and No Fun Catherine told our dominants. "I've paddled each of them multiple times with as many swats as the district allows. That's why each of you is here, to do what I can't."

Now, I was facing the wall with my hands on my head like a good girl. We didn't go so far as to give ourselves back stories, but since I am a good rule follower, I blamed the others for leading me astray. Peer pressure is a bitch, amiright? I didn't know everyone Catherine had talked into doing this, but I did know Brenna and Tommy, who was standing several "friends" down, and it was Brenna who asked, "And what exactly is that?"

"Paddle them like they deserve it. The district only allows me to administer five swats to clothed bottoms. As their parents, I expect you to do a much more thorough job on their bare behinds right here and right now, or I'll have no choice but to suspend them."

Kinda makes you wonder what happened to Catherine back in the day. I have some theories.

I won't bore you with the details, partly because I wasn't allowed to turn around. I guess I was learning by audio example, though I did have the (enjoyable) misfortune of listening with my panties around my knees and my skirt flipped part way up (that was Mary's contribution to the scene set up. Thanks, Mary!). Not that I'm an exhibitionist, but the whole humiliation thing and what I imagine were other party goers watching our predicament had me a wee bit jittery. Not my first time getting paddled at a play party or in front of others or bare in front of others, but no matter how many times, it's a rush. There are butterflies in my tummy and arousal in places and just a little bit of fear even though I'm kinda old hat at all this (wherever that expression came from).

As it happens and without me noticing it, we were lined up on the wall from tallest to not tallest, which left me at the very end, which is kind of bullshit because I'm a very tall five–foot–two. Also, I guess that was Catherine's doing. Just goes to show some people have some very particular fantasies. The tallest got to go first, so I got listen as each "parent" collected their "naughty student" and put their own spin on the scene. Certain phrases, well, I guess pretty much every spanko has certain phrases that get their motor running. I think I heard them all.

"I had to leave work early to come deal with you."

"I can't believe how you've embarrassed me."

"Wait til your father gets home."

"Who do you think you are?"

"Don't you get spanked enough at home?" (I personally like that one a lot).

"I can't believe I have to paddle you at your age."

"I thought the days of spanking your bottom were behind me."

And a lot of *young lady this* and *young man that* and "Please not here!" and "Not in front of my friends!" and "Please not bare!"

And none of that has anything to do with why I think this is the earliest sign of Mary's transformation into a big. That's all just standard school spanking scene stuff. Just about every spanko enjoys that, and it was all just to make a scene.

No, what makes me suspicious that this was a turning point is what happened when it was my turn. I listened to four other bottoms get the mischief paddled out of them. Two cried! And that wasn't because of the scene. They got paddled like spanking fetishists getting spanked by spanking fetishists, which is to say damn!!! They got it good.

I was tingly with all the feelings – nervous, excited, aroused. All the anticipation. I was practically buzzing, not to mention ready to play my part as the spunky one who takes responsibility for none of it. I was led astray by the bad ones. I'm a good girl! Let them try to make me admit my own guilt if they dare. I'd prove to them I was too strong, and I'd prove to my fiends I could take way more than they got.

"Your turn," Mary said as she took me by the elbow and turned me around. We had quite the audience, including my four battered partners in imaginary crime.

"But I didn't do anything," I said. Brat power! It's not for every Domme. It takes a special one, like Mary, to not just put up with up but handle it. I like being handled, and Mary likes to handle me (which is why she always has her hands all over me). Back to our scene …

"I don't want to hear it, Daphne Ann. I have had enough of your excuses." She swatted my butt over to the table that was serving as the principal's desk. On top of the table, Catherine's school paddle. With big drilled holes. I looked upon it with trepidation and a hankerin' for some spankerin'. What do the young people call that today? Thirst? I was parched.

"Daphne is the most willful of the five," Catherine said. "The girl is incorrigible and refuses to take responsibility for herself."

"We'll straighten that out right now." Mary sat down in one of the chairs. "Over my knee."

"Excuse me, Mrs. Taylor, but this needs to be a paddling. Please bend her over the desk like the others."

Me? I was just decoration for this part. At least at first. This was all Mary and Catherine, beginning with Mary's, "I think a firm spanking will be sufficient."

"That wouldn't be fair to the others."

"How they choose to handle their kids is their business."

"I'm afraid I have to insist."

"I know how to deal with her. Daphne, over."

"I've paddled her on three separate occasions, and none of them have gotten through. I hardly think a hand spanking will do the trick."

Standing nose to the wall with my butt hanging out for all to see? Okay. Not really self–conscious about it; I may even admit to liking it, especially since I already admitted to liking it.

Me standing there awkwardly with Mary deciding to argue her point in front of a crowd? Yeah, that got me feeling self–conscious. For one, Mary was kinda hijacking the scene, which is not very nice kink etiquette. For twosies, I felt a lot smaller than five–foot–two when Mary said, "Look at her! She's not big enough for the paddle!"

This, from a woman who had paddled me many, many times by then, including at that very event in (lovely) only recently bygone days. And I am, too, big enough for the paddle! She was only saying that to embarrass me, and it worked.

"Mary," I said under my breath, rejoining the scene as more than living (and blushing) statuary, "you're embarrassing me."

"Hush, sweetie. I'll handle this."

Before she could resume her monologue with Catherine, I interjected with, "Just paddle me."

"Honey, I said I'll handle this."

"But I am, too, big enough for the paddle." I have my pride, weird as its sources may be. Don't be telling the whole kink club I can't take the paddle! And did I mention I like getting paddled? Well, some of the time. But all the time when I'm not actually in trouble. Really. (Like, realllly. Gah! With the feelings in the places with the things. Mmmmmm.)

Catherine jumped back in with, "Even the girl knows she needs a good, hard paddling. If you didn't coddle her ..."

"How dare you!" Mary missed her calling as an actress. She'd have won an Oscar for that scene. Or at least The Golden Dildo (which is an award I just made up and now I want one ... or just gold. Just send gold ... and jewels).

"Mary, I just wanna get this over with. Just paddle me like my friends." I'd have won The Brass Butt. You know it's a good scene when you forget you're doing a scene. I started to bend myself over the table, but Mary didn't let me. She reached out and plucked me right off my feet and over her knee.

"I said no, Daphne." SPANK. "You're too little for the paddle. You'll take your spanking like a good little girl and like it!"

"I'm not too little!"

And forgetting I was in a scene, the thought of my friends making fun of me for getting spanked over Mary's knee like a kid instead of paddled flashed through my head, prompting me to try to get up (which I don't really do. Ever. Might have to chase me down sometimes and hold me still, but once I'm over a knee, I (pretty much) stay there). "My friends'll make funna me!"

"They should make fun of you! (SPANK) A girl your age behaving the way you do, you should be embarrassed. (SPANK) If you acted your age, you wouldn't need spankings at all (SPANK). But you didn't and you do, so I will put you (SPANK) over my knee (SPANK) like a little girl (SPANK SPANK) until you don't need your bottom warmed (SPANK SPANK) or until you do get big enough for the paddle (SPANK SPANK SPANK). Do you (SPANK) understand me (SPANK)?"

"Yes. Ow! I understand!"

Which is when my world got turned right side up, literally. I went from draped over Mary's knee looking at her upside-down ankles to sitting on Mary's lap looking directly into her eyes. "Do you understand why I had to spank your bare bottom?"

I about did a double take. I looked right in her eye, and yep, she was serious. That was all the spanking I was getting for the same (imaginary) misbehavior that got my friends blistered with a (nasty friggin') paddle. They had bright red and purple bruises; my butt was pink. Heck, my ears were blushing a deeper shade! And some of them really are my friends! And other friends were watching!

And a bunch of strangers were watching, but it was the friends that bothered me. They knew I could take the paddle! I can take whips and wax and chains, and they saw me get spanked and scolded like a little kid and not the fearsome, iron-bottomed warrior–brat–amazon–queen I am!

I looked away from Mary and saw people smiling and not in a way I liked. They were laughing at me! They really were making funna me!!!

And Catherine was not happy. I could see her not–happy face out of the corner of my eye as Mary stared very intently at me and I stared back. "That is not an acceptable punishment for her misbehavior," Catherine said, still thinking we had anything to do with her scene. She was mad, and people were smiling at me, and I heard someone call me adorable, and my lip started getting pouty all on its own (traitor), and Mary brushed my hair out of my face and nodded. She just nodded.

I sucked in a big breath, buried my face in Mary's sweater, and sobbed. I absolutely sobbed. Mary put one arm around my waist and the other around my shoulder so she was pressing my face into her chest and just whispered, "You're okay. Let it all out. Mary's got you."

Which is when I lost it. I bawled. Hard.

"I'll never let anyone decide how I discipline you, Daffodil. You're all mine."

Actually, nope. That was when I lost it.

"Butiwunagetaddled," I sobbed.

"That means you don't decide either, little girl. You're too little for the paddle."

"I am not," I sob–whined.

"Tonight you are, because I say you are."

Hoo boy. Had I been spanked to tears at a play party? Of course. Except this time I didn't get spanked to tears. I got embarrassed to tears, then I got loved to sobs, and then I bawled until there was snot. (You think it's funny, but it snot … I just had to say that.)

"But – hhh! – ev–er–y–one – hhh hhh – will–make–fun–a–me," I said, trying to get my breathing under control and my diaphragm to stop cramping.

"Let 'em try, Daffy. I protect you now."

Yeah, nope. *That's* when I lost it. Or lost it a third time. I don't even know.

"Is she okay," Catherine asked, having moved around to kneel down next to us.

"She's fine. She's just gotta cry it out … Told you she didn't need the paddle to learn her lesson."

Catherine, I guess, thought it would be nice of her if she reached out and patted my shoulder. Ya know how it's rude to hijack someone's scene? You do not touch someone getting aftercare. Maybe she thought that rule didn't apply because I was having a total meltdown that, to an outsider who wasn't me or Mary, looked like something much more than some scene drop, but nope. Just no. Mary has two hands, and I knew where both of them were, and feeling some strange third one made me almost knock Mary over as I, somehow, managed to get even closer to her despite already being in complete physical contact with her. She just squeezed me tighter.

"Shh shhh shhh. I got you. You're okay."

Um, she couldn't prove that. Also, I'm glad she thought so, because I didn't. I was good and freaked out by myself. In fact, I had pretty much given up any responsibility for my state of being. I stayed just like that, sitting on Mary's lap with my face buried in her shirt clinging to her and weepy, with a party going on around me and people giving us a wide berth, until Mary said, "Okay, baby. Let's get you home and into bed."

I didn't record my response for posterity, but if memory serves, I went, "Snnnnffffurlfle. Snurlf!"

"But maybe let's go to the lady's room and blow your nose first," Mary chuckled.

It was a quiet car ride home. We took a shower together for efficiency's sake and got in bed, and only after the light was out did and I could hide safely in the dark did I say, "I'm sorry."

"For what?"

"For making a scene and sobbing all over you." I didn't record it in my diary, but I'm pretty sure that was the first time I slimed her shirt.

"You don't have anything to be sorry for. I'm sorry. I didn't think you'd get so upset. I didn't mean to make you cry."

"I don't even know why."

"Was it too much," she asked. She sounded worried she'd pushed me too far, gone overboard with the humiliation. That's my Mary – she seemed so confident at the party like she knew exactly what she was doing and what I needed, but even the most confident dommes are feeling their way. A year together isn't so long. "It didn't seem like … was it something specific that got you so upset?"

"You nodded."

"When?"

"When you put me in your lap and said it was over."

"That's what set you off?"

"Put me over the edge … You nodded. I don't know why that got to me."

"How were you feeling right before I nodded?"

"Humiliated. Everyone was laughing at me."

"They were not."

"Some of them were. Why didn't you paddle me?"

"I was going to. I thought you'd sass me, and then I was going to bend you over that table. Instead your little lip started quivering, and you made sad puppy dog eyes at me."

"I was embarrassed. All those people thought I couldn't take the paddle. You spanked me like a little kid."

"Not the first time I put you over my knee."

"But everyone else got paddled. I felt … small."

"Did I hurt your feelings? I didn't mean to."

"I know. And no. Just felt … I don't know. Emotional for some reason. Did I scare you?"

"A little, at first. Everything I said just made you cry harder."

"Sorry."

"Don't be sorry. It was my fault. I guess you needed a good cry."

"You were …"

"What?"

"Being so … nice to me. Like it was okay."

"Like what was okay?"

"Bawling. Making a scene."

"Because it is okay. It's okay to cry."

"Not like that."

"Who says? You needed to. I'm just glad it was me who made you do it."

"What!? Why?"

"So I could be there to comfort you."

"I think that's what made me cry so hard."

"Me comforting you made you cry harder? Silly goose."

"It's not silly … I felt …"

"What did you feel?"

"Really loved," I said, and was kinda embarrassed to say it out loud.

"O, Daffy. That's because I really love you."

"Did you mean what you said?"

"What did I say?"

"That you protect me now."

"Of course I meant it. You're mine. That's what it means when you belong to someone."

And her saying that just made all the feelings happen. Oooof. And I thought, *we belong to each other.* "Roll over," I told her.

"Why?"

"I wanna be the big spoon."

"But you're too little," she giggled.

"Am not."

Yep, that was the turning point. According to my diary, it wasn't long after that that Mary surprised me with a pair of panties from a junior miss department. They had ponies on them, according to my records. I didn't like them, but when Mary held them out and told me to step in, I did. I didn't know that was just one of some very early baby steps toward what is today our ageplay–but–don't–call–it–that relationship.

And ever since, Mary has been my protector.

Also in my records – I AM NOT A LITTLE GIRL AND I AM NOT TOO LITTLE FOR THE PADDLE! REALLY!!! HMMMPH!!!!

Chapter 12: Happy Valentine's Day

Someone around here has to make executive decisions and take action. That's just a fact of life. You can't have just nobody taking responsibility for anything. I had to be the boss. I had to do it even without Mary's permission. Or in this case, specifically without Mary's permission because she'd said she didn't wanna do it, and there was no way not to get caught. Me taking executive action even though I knew I'd get caught? Running a risk was I. My heroism is small, but it's still heroic.

"Mary," I called out.

"What's up buttercup?"

"Could you please come help me with something?"

Okay, so I didn't so much get caught as needed to ask for help finishing what I started. I was helpful, too. I got out everything necessary to finish the job. It just looked like a different kind of job from Mary's perspective.

"Why are the stool and hairbrush in the living room? What did you do?" For the record, because I'm a recordkeeper, while I have asked for a hairbrush spanking before, I have never and will never ask for one over the stool. And don't think I didn't realize what conclusions she would draw seeing them there. I was already risking a smack bottom for what I'd started, and that was before I got out two of her favorite smack bottom accessories. Three, if you count me.

I was in the kitchen. "Promise you won't be mad?"

"Well, tell me first, and then I'll decide."

"Ugh. That is such big logic."

"Why don't you just come in here and tell me?"

"Okay … but don't be mad and don't laugh." I came out from around the corner, scissors in hand and with about one–third of a haircut. "Um, I was tired of it being so long." And she wouldn't cut it, so I forced the issue. She couldn't leave me with a third of a haircut. Now she had no choice.

"Daffy …"

"Stop giggling."

"Buh-ha!" I really need to learn to stop stomping my feet when I'm frustrated. Half the time it just gets me in trouble, and the other half it makes Mary go, "Aww. You're adorable."

"Would you please help me finish?"

"I guess we don't have any choice now. Come sit." I got on the stool and remembered there's a reason I don't like stools – I feel like a little kid when I sit on them. I know no one's feet touch the floor when they're sitting on a stool, but when I sit on one, I'm so short I have to hop–scoot my way up to the bar (or else ask Mary to subtly push me in). Makes me feel like I'm in a highchair. So when you go out with friends again and you go to a bar, just be courteous and don't sit at the bar if your friends are under five–seven.

"Have you ever actually sat on this," Mary asked.

"Not really what we bought it for, is it?"

"Well, I don't know, Daffy. It is a stool. What did we buy it for then?"

"Grumble."

"I don't think we bought it for grumble. I think we bought it for me to sit on when you go over the knee."

Over the knee – makes it sound like *on the chopping block.*

She was trying to needle me, so I reminded her, "Haircut."

"And more specifically," Mary said while hugging me from behind. She likes, um, doing stuff to me from behind, "we got it because nothing reminds you what a little girl you are than being put over my knee on this stool so your handsies and feetsies don't even touch the floor. Doesn't that make you feel all helpless and submissive?"

"Marrry."

"Got a picture of what we're going for?" I took out my phone and brought up the picture of the haircut I was trying to give myself.

"Hmm. Maybe next time something a little less complicated."

"Think you can do it?"

"I can do the amateur version. You did a pretty good job getting started."

"Does that mean you're proud of me?"

"Of course I am." Heehee! My wife is proud of me. "O look," she said, "Daffy went fishing for compliments and caught one."

"Ha!"

"I'm gonna miss your long hair. I liked styling it. Head up."

"Maybe it'll be back in a few months. I just don't like having to take care of it."

"I see. So if I promised to wash it and comb it for you, would you grow it back out?"

"Like every day?"

"Mhmm."

"Heh. Maybe."

"Every night before bed you could sit in front of me while I brush your hair one hundred times."

"You are such a big."

"And you are not saying no, so what does that make you?"

"A woman of few words."

"That's a fib if ever I heard one."

"So you saw the stool and hairbrush and thought I got them out so you could spank me?"

"It's what they're for."

"Yeah, but why did you think I spread newspaper on the floor."

"In case you piddled while getting your bottom spanked."

"Marrrry. When have I ever piddled while getting my bottom spanked? And who even does that?"

"Well, then do you care to explain why when I take down your undies to spank that cute little bottom of yours, they're so often damp?"

Eep. "No. No, I do not care to explain that." She kissed my cheek from behind. And was that ear nibble? Heehee!

"One thing I do like about your short hair," Mary said.

"What's that?"

"It so much easier to nibble on your earlobe."

Ooo, a warm and tingly sensation in my tummy. "You keep saying stuff like that and I'm gonna start thinking you like me and stuff," I warned her.

"Hold up your phone again."

Imagine going to the stylist and the stylist not having a mirror in front of you for you to watch. Now, swap out the stylist for an IT developer (or whatever Mary's title is). It's an exercise in faith, supported by remembering no one but the IT developer is really gonna see you for a while (besides from the grandma next door and your parents on zoom).

"Did I ever tell you," Mary asked, "that one of the only real spankings I ever got growing up was for cutting my own hair?"

"I can see where you're going with this." She's as subtle as a toaster (just think about that and you'll realize it's a perfectly good simile).

"Mom was not happy with me," Mary said.

"How old were you?"

"Ummm, I think kindergarten?"

"You sure she wasn't mad because you were playing with scissors?"

Mary stopped what she was doing for a second. "Well, now I'm not … she … hmm."

"I'm insightful like that." She gave me another kiss on the cheek.

"We're going to need to wash your hair when we're done," she said. "Get all the stray bits."

"I know. We should do that in the downstairs bathroom."

"Why?"

"Reasons." I have reasons. Like that tub is big enough for both of us, and I already got the bath beads ready and some champagne and strawberries chilling in the back of the fridge.

"Silly goose."

"I'm not a silly goose."

"Then what are you?"

"I'm your funny valentine … Mary?"

"(Sniff)."

"Aww, please don't do that." Whenever she does it, I end up doing it, like, thirteen times harder.

"(Kiss)." Ooo, heehee. The back of my neck. The rest of my neck. Shoulder. Ear. Kiss kiss kiss kiss. *Sigh...*

"Happy Valentine's Day, Mary."

"Happy Valentine's Day, Daffodil."

Chapter 13: Bottles and Bribery

Cold? Us too, but not as cold as lots of other places. It was just cold enough for us to go hiking and come back ruddy cheeked and wanting hot food, ideally prepared by someone else, served after a hot shower which we took together to be efficient and to save water and to reach places we can't reach on our own. Really.

Mary combed my hair (what's left of it) and sent me toward the bedroom with a swat to my butt through the towel I was wearing. "Wait for me," she said. Not that I didn't want all the sex, but also dinner. It's like my mom always said, at least make 'em buy you dinner first. Or perhaps mom didn't say that. Doesn't sound like her. Maybe it was my older cousin. Family rumor has it she got lots of free dinners, which I still wanna believe means she's good at couponing because I am an innocent.

Anyhoo, Mary emerged from our bathroom in her robe as I observed from flat on my back on the bed, wondering what she wanted me to wait for. And was it *wait* as in don't go anywhere or *wait* as in don't get dressed or *wait* as in don't start nuthin' without her? Not that I've ever been known to start anything without her … anyhoo …

She chuckled at me and said, "You got that look you get from fresh air."

"I'm an avid outdoorswoman, within a narrow band of meteorological conditions." The rest of the time, I'm an avid couchwoman. "And you're one to talk, telling me to wait for you to do things to me."

"Who said anything about doing things to you? I just wanna get you dressed," she said as she took her robe off and started to get dressed.

"Could you do that thing again," I asked.

"What thing?"

"That thing where you bend forward to put your foot through your pant leg." I don't know why I like that. Just ... her body. I like to watch it move. Also, if she did it again, she'd have to get undressed first, and I can work with that.

"See anything else you like," she asked.

"You. But just to be clear, that would be a no on the sex with you putting clothes on?"

"Well, for now. I gotta eat."

O yeah, I was just thinking about that. I got distracted by Mary. She's always distracting me with shiny objects, like her body. And this one time, she got a belly button ring and I was so distracted that I forgot go to work for a week.

"What are we gonna order," I asked.

"Hold on." She disappeared for just a second as she put a big flannel shirt on. Grey leggings, flannel shirt. She thinks she dresses very conservatively, but when she does that thing where she pulls the shirt down and takes her hair out of the collar ...

"Mmmm," I said as I put my head back on the bed.

"What," she chuckled.

"Nothin'."

I was that good kind of tired when you feel just at ease with the world and content to be with your person, and Mary made her are–you–happy face before asking,

"Are you happy?" See? Mary and me are on the same wave length. I nodded.

"And now you're sleepy? First, she wants food; then she wants sex; then she wants food; then she wants to fall asleep," Mary narrated. "Let's get you dressed."

"Can I wear this," I asked and yawned.

"I think we can do better than a wet towel."

She disappeared into the closet, and it was my turn to sigh. "I know what you're getting."

"If you didn't have a darn good idea by this point, I'd be questioning how smart you are," she said as she came back out. "Besides, it's cold."

"Did they teach you non–sequiturs like that in domme school?"

"Did they teach smartass questions like that in brat school?"

"I'm self–taught." I could start my own school … And since I'm thinking of going back to school to be a teacher … Do they give credit for life experience?

"Now I get to unwrap my present," Mary said as she loomed over me (she's always looming over me, bedeviling me, beguiling me and besmirching my honor in the best ways) and opened my towel. "Aww, just what I always wanted."

"What part? I need some specifics." Because if she wants me to keep going along with the ageplay and diaper thing, I'm gonna need some flattery. Like, *all the compliments, please*. But I'm only saying please to be polite. It's not a request. Really.

"I think," she said pretending to be thinking with her finger on her chin making a thinking face. I can't even make a thinking face around here anymore without getting accused of peeing my pants. "I like this part best," she said and bent down to kiss my tummy.

"Heehee. Mary, I'm ticklish."

"Ya don't say? What with me having tickled you into submission before, I'd have never guessed." *Sigh ...* "And look what I got for you." *Groan ...*

"Where do you even find this stuff," I asked as she showed me a diaper with farm animals on it.

"You can always pick out your own," she said as she unfolded it.

"That would be construed as participation, and I refuse to participate in my own mistreatment," I said as I lifted my hips because reasons and had an existential panic moment of questioning how it was that I could participate in my own mistreatment while simultaneously refusing to do exactly that. *Stupid brain pointing out the conflicts between my words and actions like anybody even asked it.* Anyhoo, "And doesn't anyone make any that are at least not so cutesy?"

"There's the medical ones."

"... Those are ugly ... Not that it matters because I hate them all." I took a chance and lifted my head to see her making her skeptical face. Being skeptical at me just because my words don't match my actions... *grumble.* "Don't you be looking at me like that. Shouldn't you be massaging things into places?"

"Was that you telling me to get back to work," she said all o so eager to snark at me. "And wouldn't that make you the boss of this diapering?"

"No. It would not," I pouted (like a boss).

"So," she said, "you're just concerned what would happen if you went peepee in your diapee without any diaper rash cream on, is that it," she said as she applied said cream.

"That's not it at all. I … hhh! I just …" *Don't squirm. Don't give her the satisfaction.*

"You're looking a little red there, Daff."

"Where? Gonna hafta to be a lot more specific." Because there were rednesses. Multi–redness. Places plural were red.

"Well," she said, "not in your pretty windburnt cheeks." Her hands went away, and then I felt her closing that diaper over me. "After such a chilly day, wouldn't some oatmeal feel good?"

"O don't even," I said, holding my hands up so she could help me sit up. I looked down at myself and sighed.

"What pattern would be acceptable to you, then," Mary asked me.

"Something cool … fractals. Or more grown up, like lewd imagery. Or zoning laws."

"Good thing you're not a silly goose, or someone would accuse you of being a silly goose. Up up."

"Up up?" What's 'up up'?

"On your feetsies."

"And you can't just say that because," I asked.

"Are you grumpy? Because I don't wanna have to adjust any attitudes tonight."

"I'm not grumpy. I m … inquisitive. And really, with the footie pajamas," I inquired.

"Really. And you know what they say about people who are inquisitive?"

"Nope. Never heard it," I deadpanned. "Did they teach you what people say about people who are inquisitive when you were in domme school?"

"Ah," she scoffed. "Just for that, ya little smart mouth, the dropseat can stay down all night." For the record, the dropseat footie pajamas predate the ageplay stuff. She just wanted quick access to my butt once, and lo and behold, one day I received dropseat pajamas as a Happy Tuesday gift, and I beheld. Later on, as in mere minutes later on, Mary beheld my butt as I stood in the corner with my red buns hanging out.

When she zipped me up and unbuttoned the flap, she gave me a pat on the butt and sighed. "That sigh was suspiciously wistful," I said.

"You look pretty," she said.

"Um, thank you." I suspected a but.

"But I wouldn't mind having some of that pretty red hair back to braid."

I turned around. "It could come back if it would make you happy." I put my arms around her neck.

"It's your hair, though," she said.

"You may not have noticed, Mary, but, um, I do a lot of stuff mainly because it makes you happy." *Crinkle.*

"Uh–huh. Just me."

"Yes. What do you want for dinner. I'll order."

"Whatever you're having. I'll go make us some drinks."

"Make mine full of alcohol," I said as I turned and collected another pat on the butt. Butt pats feel good. Everyone should have at least three a day. But diaper pats are … different … somehow.

I went downstairs, being very careful on the stairs lest the soles of these footies fly out from under me and send me to the land of quadriplegia (like, seriously, people put these on their kids!?!), cracked the window behind the couch to let some of that cool air in, turned on the fireplace to balance it out, flopped onto the sofa, and got out my phone. "Is Italian okay," I called out to my wife the bartendress.

"Perfect. And order a salad."

"Tiramisu," I called out.

"A salad!"

"Tirami–salad," said I and ordered both along with some pasta. See, the thing about tiramisu is – and this is why I ordered three overpriced pieces – is that as good as it is, it's even better when I eat it off of Mary's finger because she, um, tastes yummy. Not that I had any designs on the evening with the intent of luring her into feeding my tiramisu off her finger on the way to … other activities.

"What are we gonna watch," I asked as I got the remote out and the blanket. You might call it nesting … love nesting. Teehee!

"Something we haven't seen before," Mary said as she waltzed into the living room like the queen of the waltzing floor.

"Where's mine," I said when I only saw one glass in her hand.

"It's right here," her queenship said as she revealed …

"Awww. Marryyyy!"

"It's been two whole months since Christmas, and we haven't used your Christmas present once," she said with The Royal Smirk plastered to her face. "Don't you want your baba?"

"No."

She sat down on the couch next to me. "But I made this just for you."

"Which I appreciate, but I want it in a glass."

"What's wrong with drinking from a bottle?"

"All the things."

"O, but you don't mind eating tiramisu off my finger." So she knew that was going to happen. Wonder how she guessed (past experience; lots of past experience).

"That's ... different. And in the future." Seventy–five minutes, according to the app. We should've ordered in advance. "I want to be in the present, Mary. All my therapists and all the mindfulness apps have always said I should live in the present." She laid her head back against the arm of the couch with that smirk still there, like she'd already won. But she hadn't. No. No winner her.

"And in the present, I really think you should lay your head back right here," she said, touching her ... chest, "and open wide for your baba."

"... What's in it?"

"A cosmo."

"Why?"

"Because you like cosmos."

"No, I mean why?"

"Is it important?"

"Sort of ... yes."

"Well, we've talked about it before."

True, but, "And it still ... I wanna talk more." I wasn't satisfied with the previous talks, not if she now wanted to introduce feeding me from a bottle and didn't think, o, that I might want to understand why she wants to do that to me. With me. Both?

"Can we talk in the morning after church," she asked.

"Promise?"

"Of course, Daffy."

Hmmm. "What will you give me?"

"For what?"

"For drinking out of that thing."

"Hmmmm." She made her thinking face again. "Well, how about instead of you eating tiramisu off my finger, I eat it off you?"

Deal. "Gimme my drink."

"Ha! Lay back." Which I did, but not because I liked it. Because she bribed me with sex. Which is very dignified in ways some might not understand. "One day I'll even let you drink out of this yourself, but you're gonna hafta use two hands."

"Just for that, I'm gonna need specifics," I stipulated.

"Specifics?" I settled back and she stroked my hair.

"Which parts of me will you be eating tiramisu off of? I need details."

"Open up, and I'll tell you all about it."

"Like I've never heard that before …" If she was just trying to get me drunk and pliable, she coulda chosen a different nipple … That came out wrong. "It won't come." … Also came out wrong.

"You hafta press it with your tongue before you suck … Why are you blushing? … For someone who hates this so much, you sure are laughing pretty hard … What?"

"I'll – ha! Hahaha! Mmmm. I'll tell you later."

"My pretty happy girl." She gave me a forehead kiss. *Sigh…*

Chapter 14: The Underpants Gnome

It was Mary's idea. Well, in a loose sense that she made an off handed comment that made my ears perk up and I thought to myself, *self, you can have some pandemic fun with that.*

I would've let the idea go, too, except Mary keeps moving my laundry. I do the laundry, I put away the laundry, I go to don some of my laundry, and in one particular drawer I don't find said laundry that I know I put there. Not all the time, but when it comes to panties, that's something you really need all the times you go looking.

Not that going commando is the worst thing (I could totally be a commando if the criteria were how often and well one goes commando), but in my effort to not succumb to complete pandemic sloppiness, I'm trying to wear actual clothes. Mary is not helping that effort when she takes panties out of my drawer and replaces them with a diaper. Her pre–pandemic delight in buying me panties from the junior miss section led to me having way too many panties, and I don't know where all those went. I do know that I'm down to maybe three of those and two regular pair, and that's not enough when it's laundry day and she decides it would be hilarious to leave me with none to wear.

I don't even know what she's trying to accomplish. Unless she's just trying to make sure I never don't feel at least a little teased. It's like bratting in reverse, now that I think on it, and yeah, putting up with a brat is hard. I felt, shall we say, a little competitive, like no one was going to out brat me.

Bratting is an art form. Newbies go rushing in there with *the look at me look at me I'm misbehaving look at me* approach, and there's a time and a place for that, but some art needs to build slowly, such as over the course of a laundry cycle, by which I do not mean the machine but the days that pass between loads of laundry. That's why I don't call this The Great Panty Raid. I call it The Panty Embezzlement.

"Daffy," Mary called to me (she's always calling to me) one wonderful afternoon after her post–workout shower, "is there clean laundry in the dryer?"

"No," I called back, "I did it yesterday." Another hard part of being a brat and staying true to your art? Not getting so eager that you don't let things play out in their natural time. So rather than run upstairs to speed up these events, I waited. And waited. And took off my pants and got under a blanket. And waited until Mary came back downstairs.

"Are you sure you got all the laundry," she asked as she came downstairs, wearing (I'm guessing because pants) the thong I left her (she's not a fan; your butt cheeks belong together, she once told me, cuz your butt cheeks are friends).

"Mhmm." Yep, I got it all. O, I got it all (*evil cackle*).

"You couldn't have," she said as she headed toward our main floor laundry (woohoo! main floor laundry; gotta get excited about the little things these days).

"I keep our house very well, thank you very much." *Let's see who can gaslight who better.* "If you don't like the way I do the chores, maybe you should start doing your own laundry." Yeah, that's risky and likely to only end one way, but it was worth the risk.

"I didn't mean it that way. I just … can't find anything." I waited. I am a patient huntress (sometimes; almost never, actually, but this time I was feeling like I could play the long game, delayed gratification being the mark of a mature soul and all that, especially when it was only likely to be delayed a few minutes).

I heard the dryer door open again. "Could you come help me look, please?"

I hopped out from under my camouflage (blanket) and headed toward our main floor laundry (woohoo! main floor laundry!) and leaned against the edge of the door frame. "Did you check the hamper," I asked. "It's not like I'm hiding your panties." Because we're sympatico, I and only I could see the little lightbulb flick on above her head. Shut went the dryer drawer, up came Mary from her (wonderful) bent over posture, and pivot she did on her foot to look me right in the eye.

"Daphne Ann, what did you … Are you wearing my panties?"

Her hands were inspecting my wardrobe before I could utter, "Don't be ridiculous."

Smack! Worth it. "Explain yourself, young lady."

"Possession is ninth tenths of the law, Mary." That shut her up. "And pbbbbbt!" Yep, I raspberried her. *This is gonna hurt. So worth it.*

"You (spank) are in (spank) over (spank spank) your head (spank spank spank spank spank)."

"Lemme go! Ow!" She thinks she's always got the upper hand because she spanks me with her hand, but I got game, too. "I just wanna wear pretty panties like you!" *And cue the sad puppy eyes.*

Had she accused me of being full of shit, she wouldn't have been wrong. But if she can start kinky sex games, I can too. You might even say I started the very first one. After all, who was letting her butt get passed around at a spanking party when Mary found it? Little ol' me, that's who.

Her right hand paused in midair while her left kept its gentle grip around my arm, not that I was trying to get away. "Upstairs," she said, and walked us upstairs, notably without any more spanks to my butt. Perhaps she just didn't want to damage her panties. Ha! I got spanked on Mary's panties. Mary's panties got a spanking. Heeheehee!

"You're in trouble. Stop smiling," she ordered me.

"No." And ya know what? "Make me."

Into the bedroom we went, and she sat down on the ottoman. She doesn't sit on the ottoman often. Usually just when she intends to paddle me silly, so I may have bitten off more than I could chew. But always a chance not.

"What is this," she said, taking my panties (right then is when I decided they're mine) and snapping the waistband.

"I like them … Mine." *Heeheeheeheehee!* She looked quizzical, one might say.

"But … what are you … Explain yourself, young lady."

"You said that already." *SMACK! And cue the crocodile tears.* "I just wanna look pretty and wear panties like yours."

"But they're not yours."

"But all my pretty ones are missing." *End crocodile tears.* "And you can have yours back when I get mine back." *Booyah!* And then I went *yoink* like a cartoon getting yoinked over Mary's knee and collected six or twenty, give or take, rapid fire spanks.

"You do not take things that do not belong to you."

"Looks who's talking! OW! You took all my good ones!"

"*Your* good ones?" *SPANK!* She left her hand there. "You don't have any panties, honey."

"Yes I do, and you've been taking them and putting them somewhere."

"I took my panties, that I bought for you to wear, and left you the ones I want you to wear."

"But ... I bought most of those ... I used to have a job, ya know." I had my own money. It's all been spent now, but that is not relevant.

"It doesn't matter who paid for them, sweetie. I own them."

"You ..." I twisted around to give her one heck of a dirty look. "Whatever happened to equal partners?"

"We are equal partners, Daffy, but this is mine," she said and took a handful of butt. My butt, not hers. "Which means everything that goes in it or on it is mine." She took her hand off my butt, placed it back on the part of me that's not quite my butt and isn't quite my front, and said, "That's just the natural order of things." Motions ... in placed. "Besides, you look so silly, like you're wearing your big sister's panties."

"I do not … gggg ... look silly. I … pretty." Words were hard to come by with her hands doing that thing to the places.

"So silly and pretty. These don't fit you. They're much too big for you."

"But I like them," I managed to say.

"But you're just a little girl. You're not grown up enough to wear … … Daffy?"

… Well, that was unexpected …

"Daffy, did you just cum in your undies?"

" … … … … Um, they're not mine? Woah!" She ninjaed me like a griddle cake, flipped me right over so I was sitting on her knee. "Hi." *Teehee.*

"You're in for it now," she said, looking quite amused.

"Uh–huh," said I. "You, um, you know your hand is still, um … handing." Ooh, I made a word … and stuff. She took her hand away. *Awwww, consarnit!*

"First you go snooping in my drawers."

"Ha! Guhaha. Haahaaaahaaa (snort). Snooping … (snort) … in your … ha! Hahaha! (snort) … drawers (snort) because the double (snort) mee–meaning (snort) … hmmmmm."

Mary was trying so hard to not crack up. "Then you. A–ha–hem! Then you take things that don't belong to you and you …" She was turning purple holding in a belly laugh. "You do a number three in my panties."

Well, that was fun while it lasted. "A what now?"

"This little underpants rebellion of yours is over, little missy. You will wear what I put in your drawer for you to wear."

"But ... I ... Mary, I like my things. I wanna wear ... I'm a woman. I like wearing pretty things."

"I know you're a woman, and you're a beautiful one, but you don't decide what goes on that part of you anymore." She was about to put her hand back on that part of me and appeared to think better of it, possibly because ... anyhoo.

"Since when is that a rule?"

"Hmmm, since a while, but officially, now."

"But ... Mary, I wanna ..."

"And you can, when I say."

"And when is that?"

"Often enough to make you happy. How's that?"

"Vague."

"Mhmm. You behave better when you're on your toes. And you won't be wearing any undies for at least two days. Guess what you're wearing for the next two days."

"Guayabera shirt?"

"Nope."

"Why two days?"

"For your two offenses."

"What two? I don't count two." *Pout.*

"Fibbing and being an underpants gnome."

If anyone in our house is an underpants gnome, it's Mary! "I am not an underpants gnome!"

"The gnomiest."

"Marrrry!"

"You just did a number three in your undies, and you know the rule about number one. Do you need a rule about number two, or will you admit you're just a little underpants gnome who stole panties that are not appropriate for such a little girl?"

Grrr. And nope never! And grrr. "Gnome," I meeped.

"And look at what you did when you tried to wear grownup undies," she said. If I did what she did next, she'd have asked me, *do we look with our hands or with our eyes?*

"I regret nothing."

"You know who cums in their undies during a spanking?"

"Eager little beavers whose wives are … d–doing what (gulp) you're d–doing now?"

"Big girls can hold it for …"

Barely long enough to move to the bed.

AND I AM NOT AN UNDERPANTS GNOME! She is! I want my panties back!

But she can have back the pair I borrowed. I, um, don't want them anymore. Because reasons.

Chapter 15: I Needed a Damn Hug

I don't want to talk about it anymore. I can't mourn my grandma in this stupid pandemic. It was a complicated relationship, and I mostly just feel bad for my dad, who doesn't do bad emotions very well, on top of which he is totally freaked out by mortality. That's what's bugging me most, is that I can't go to him. He needs me, and I can't go because of this stupid pandemic.

Mary has been an angel, of course, because she is an angel in addition to being a ninja, sorceress, coyote, queen, and something with computers. If I blink loud enough, she'll come and ask me if I need anything. I think maybe deep down she wants me to be more upset. Or maybe not that deep down. She thinks I'm holding it in and that that won't end well, plus she likes to take care of me. But really, like I said, I'm not ready to mourn. Better to wait and do it right all at once than do some now and some when I can go home and see my parents.

Though I guess I've been doing the hedonistic parts of mourning, self–medicating with sugar, sleep, and too much laying around. I know that's not good, but as I remind myself, it's a process, and I need to be extra forgiving with myself (I'm good at that). Later on, I can be extra not forgiving with myself (I'm awesome at that), but for now, I got all the way to the end of Netflix and spent forty dollars having a platter of cookies delivered to me. I don't feel like baking (I know, but don't be scared; I'm alright; really; I think).

At least Spring is almost here. That's got me in sophomore gardening mode. I made a map of my garden in google sheets, and each cell is something I'm planting.

Won't be long now until the bulbs I planted last year come up. Too bad the order you do things in in the garden matters. I wanna go buy a bunch of mulch and spread it just to give me something to do. Yep, no weird mourning feelings there. Really … sigh …

"Daffodil," Mary called to me as she came from wherever she was.

"I'm in here," I said from our living room couch. Maybe it's the pandemic talking, but I'm starting to have weird, tingly feelings for that thing my butt spends so much time on.

"How you feeling," she asked when she got to me.

"I'm okay."

"I got a surprise for you," she said.

"I like surprises. Wuddya get me?" *Ding–dong* went the doorbell.

"There it is."

"Is it tacos, by chance," I asked because reasons (which is tacos; yep, I'm good at the hedonist part of mourning, and we're just going to all agree to pretend it's mourning and not a continuation of my stress eating since forever).

"Better." She looked positively bouncy as she bounced off the sofa. I heard her open our front door, and then the door closed and she poked her head around the corner. "You have a visitor."

Mary came back into the living room wearing her mask and tossed me my own. I haven't been around anyone but Mary since before Christmas. No one has been in our home but us since before Christmas.

"Mary," I said, wondering just how out of her mind she was. She'd been twice as paranoid as I was, and

I was friggin' paranoid! I mean, I know she wanted to do something nice for me, but I didn't want someone in our house. And a little warning woulda been nice so I could at least put on real clothes. "I can't," I said. I was a little miffed. Like, this shoulda been a joint decision.

"It's me," Nana said from our entryway. And there was Nana, also wearing a mask.

"She's had both her shots and quarantined for ten days," Mary said. "We wanted to surprise you."

I was all bouncy as I bounced off the couch, but I didn't scurry over to her. I just stood up. I mean, we'd talked on the phone and by text and over the fence. I hadn't told her about my grandma yet.

"Hi. Um, is this a good idea," I asked.

"I quarantined," Nana repeated.

"Well, that was nice of you," I said. "You didn't see your kids?" Not that I was investigating. Just that if she went ten days without seeing her kids and grandkids, that was super nice of her.

"Nope."

"How about we all sit down instead of being so awkward," Mary suggested. Like I'm ever awkward … Okay, but Mary isn't. She drips steely confidence. My awkwardness just sometimes rubs off on her.

"Did you quarantine just for me," I asked as I took my rightful place on my new BFF with benefits, a/k/a the sofa.

"Mhmm. I wanted to see you guys." She sat next to me. "And I'm hoping you and I can get started on our gardens soon."

"I have a plan," I told her.

"I can't wait to see it. How's everything else? You guys doing okay," she asked me. Ugh, such a loaded question. I think we shouldn't ask that question anymore until 2022.

"Daffy," Mary asked me when I didn't respond right away. And maybe because my lip started trembling. Actually, you know what it was? It was probably the tears spilling out of my eyes.

"No," is all I said. And social distancing rules be damned. I hugged Nana.

Chapter 16: Of All the Things to Be Addicted To …

"You've been using again," Mary accused me. She is just so melodramatic sometimes.

"I have not. I just … ugh," I said because I was dizzy.

"You have. Where did you get it?"

"I didn't. I just don't feel well."

"I can see that. I know what it looks like. We beat this, Daffy. Remember? We beat this. Tell me the truth: are you using again?"

"I … yes. But only a little, Mary. Just a little. And it feels so good!"

"It doesn't matter. It's too much. Look at you – you're all flushed and dizzy." She sighed. "I think we have to take you to the clinic."

"I don't wanna go."

"I don't want you to go, either, but I'm not sure they'll call in a prescription without seeing you."

"Let's call Dr. Murray." My immunologist. She'd call in a prescription. She wouldn't want me risking covid at urgent care for just an ear infection.

"I'll call. You go get the Q–tips you're not supposed to buy and bring them down here."

Okay, so I have – had! – this bad habit of using Q–tips, which ironically make your ears itch more but feel sooo good! And if you're prone to ear infections, sometimes using them gives you an ear infection, so Mary made me stop using them. It was a struggle (they feel sooooo good!). It says right on the box not to put them in your ears. Must be the object most used for the thing you're specifically not supposed to use them for. I get all jonesing for it for days after I stop using them, but it goes away and stops itching.

I went and got them, was sorely tempted to stash a few for emergencies, but resisted and went back downstairs to find Mary on hold to talk to a nurse. She held out her hand and took the box. I sat down next to her.

"Hi," Mary said into her phone. "I'm hoping to get some antibiotics called in for my wife. She has an ear infection … No, she hasn't been seen, but she gets them often enough to know, and I don't want to take her to urgent care and be around people who might have covid … Her ear hurts, she's dizzy …" Mary reached out and put the back of her hand to my forehead. "She's running a temperature. Doesn't feel too high … Thank you. We appreciate it … She's fine otherwise. I'm keeping her close to home. We've been very careful … Thank you. You, too."

Mary hung up and pivoted her chair. "She'll call back in an hour. In the meantime …" I saw where that was going and stood up and started pushing my pajama bottoms down to go over Mary's lap. She stopped me.

"Mmm–mmm," she said. "I think you're learning your lesson already. Besides, I don't spank little girls when they're sick." Well, that's just not true because past times … but I didn't feel like reliving the past right then.

"I'm sorry."

"You look sorry. Come on." She took my hand.

"Where are we going?"

"To put you back to bed." We went upstairs, into our bedroom, and into the bathroom. "But a cool bath first will make you feel better. Arms up."

I put my arms up because Mary is a robber who's always telling me to put my arms up and then steals my shirt. But at least she asks. She rarely asks when she steals my pants. She ran the tub while I stood there being naked, which is an activity even if most people don't think it is. Mary put her hand in the water to test the temperature, and I stepped in. It was tepid at best. I wanted a hot bath (I always want a hot bath), but that would make me feel worse.

"Lean forward," Mary said, and I did and drew my knees up under me, put my arms around them, and rested my chin against them as Mary washed my back. "Of all the self–destructive habits you could have, this must be the most adorable in a silly way. Addicted to Q–tips ..."

"I don't always get ear infections."

"Nope, but often enough. You do know most adults almost never get an ear infection at all, right?"

"Yeah."

"And you know what that makes you, right?"

"I'm not a little girl," I said weakly. "Ahh!" Ear infections are sneaky. It's a dull ache, and then all of a sudden there's a sharp pain for a couple seconds.

"Such a silly girl. Does the water feel good?"

"Mhmm, but it's cold."

"Almost done. Arms up."

Ooo, soap and hands and soapy hands went all over the place. Too bad I didn't feel good enough to really enjoy it. Mary was true to her word and started keeping a small pitcher under the sink for washing my hair. She filled it with fresh water. "I'll be very careful," she promised and poured just a little in my hair at a time, just enough to get it wet without getting any in my ear.

She reached over to pull the plug, and I started to stand before she told me, "Sit."

"I'm not that dizzy."

"Are you not not dizzy? Then you can keep your bottom on the bottom of the tub." She pulled a towel off the bar and waited until the water was gone. "So many goose bumps. Up we go." She helped me stand, wrapped the towel around me, and steered me in front of the mirror. I stood still while she combed my hair. When she was done, she wrapped an arm around my belly, put her chin on my shoulder, gave me a kiss on the neck, and said, "I'm sorry you don't feel well," and gave me another kiss. "If you ever put one of those in your ear again …" She didn't finish the sentence. Or she did, but with a couple of firm pats of the hairbrush to my betowelled butt, which she then un–betowelled and hung the towel back up.

Back to the bedroom we went, where Mary pointed to the bed. I sat and watched her get a cloth diaper out of the closet and some of those plastic panties. "Lay back, Daffy. We have a brand-new rule to discuss."

"Do I get to discuss it," I asked. Because not all of our discussions about rules involve discussing.

"Not really. Lift." I lifted, and she situated. "If you're sick, you're in diapers."

"O." She sprinkled powder on my parts. Whenever she does that, she always gets a little on my tummy. I think she does that on purpose. She likes to rub it in. I like it when she rubs it in, but then I just like tummy rubs. And I swear I'm not a golden retriever. Really.

"You want jammies," she asked.

"No."

"You won't be too cold?"

"Mmm–mmm." I swear I'm not pathetic when I'm sick. I'm just monosyllabic sometimes when I'm sick.

"Under the covers with you then." She lifted the covers, and I slid in, then she slid in behind me.

"Don't you have to work," I asked her.

"Yeah."

"You should probably go do that then."

"Such a bossy pants for someone wearing diapers."

"I can be bossy in anything … when you let me." I sure wish she'd let me be bossy more.

"You can be the boss of pants piddling whenever you're in a diaper."

"Marrry! Be nice to me. I'm ahhh! (*sniff*)."

"Getting worse?"

"Mhmm."

"Aren't natural consequences the worst?"

"Yes. Mary?"

"Mhmm?"

"This sucks." Me and my stupid addictions. Sugar, Q–tips, peanut butter. The only good addiction is Mary.

"I know, sweetie. I'm sorry."

"Thanks for taking care of me."

"You're very welcome. I like taking care of you."

Chapter 17: Springtime

I'll admit Mary was onto something when she looked at me hopping out of bed in the morning and called me a happy Daffy. And why? Because Springtime! I used to say fall was my favorite season, and last year during quarantine I realized it was spring. Might've had something to do with being outside during the day for the first time since I started working, but spring, I realized, is awesome.

It's even better this year because I have my garden to play in. It really is kinda awesome that you can plant a bulb in the fall and get a flower in the spring. Tulips! And of course, daffodils. Shoot, I'm so giddy I kinda wanna get a little sunburned, just a smidge, to kick off the season.

Now, there's also some sadness as Brenna isn't having her annual pool party, but last year that event seriously did not go in my favor. Things were done to me. But I have a surprise for Mary, whose office is on the first floor, which makes it o so fun to knock on her window. "Can you come out and play," I asked.

She swiveled in her chair and gave me one of those aww-isn't-she-cute looks she's always giving me. She opened the window, and said, "What's up, buttercup?"

"I got a surprise for you."

"I got a call in four minutes, but …"

"It's a pool!" So I might not be good at holding in surprises. "I bought a pool."

"You … better not have." She looked confused.

"It's inflatable, silly. They sold out last year, so I ordered one at Christmas time. It just got here."

"Where's it gonna go?"

"It'll fit on the patio. Just a place to cool off when it gets hot … and maybe a place to get bizzay when things get hot?"

"Did you really just say 'get bizzay'?" If anyone can bring back that phrase, it's me, so she can shhh!

"I ... may have. Also, you need to spank me later."

"Why?"

"The spending limit rule. I broke it like, seven ... no, nine times."

"On a kiddie pool!"

"No; on landscaping, but I told you proactively, so I get in less trouble."

"Daphne Ann!"

"You're late for your call."

"You're in for it after work. Just you ... wait til I get home, I suppose."

Ha! Mary's flustered! Let her be the flustered one for once. Not that I'm ever flustered because I'm not, and also, it's springtime! Perhaps I've been a little cooped up. Which is not the same as being a little who has been cooped up so don't even with your wordplay that you're not even as good at as me.

Said landscaping had, mostly, not arrived, but according to the internet, the beds must be prepared for planting, so I got to work on doing that. I tore out dead stuff, cleaned out leaves, turned over dirt, found what may have been a snake hole and put a rock on top of it, and got all the potted plants from out of the garage and arrayed them on our porch in the sunshine. Either they're potted plants that are dormant, or they're just pots full of dirt and the remains of dead plants. Time will tell – how exciting!

I don't know what Mary was doing. Earning money for me to spend, I suppose. I know a thing or two about shareholder capitalism, and I think getting the money without doing the work makes me the boss, but I don't think I should say so.

And dirt! It feels good to get on your knees in the dirt and work it with your hands. So much better than the sanitized reality I've been living in all winter. I'm going to make broccoli come right out of the ground. How is that not so much cooler than anything else? But for the time being, I just made piles of yard waste I needed to dispose of the next day. I was content with my day's work and laid down on the grass, still a little damp despite the clear day, as the sun went down and just enjoyed the coolness. Sigh … springtime, renewal, all that poetic crap.

"You're filthy," was what my darling spouse had to say to me from above.

"I'm showing the evidence of my labor," I countered.

"Let's get you cleaned up." She held out both her hands and helped me to my feet, and once I was on my feet, she assaulted me!

Okay, overly dramatic, but, "Ow! What was that for?" She just goes and smacks my butt without stating the reason like she doesn't know I'm the boss or something. "Ow!"

"I'm just brushing the dirt off you."

"Ow! Marrry! I'm not a rug."

"You're right, we should get a carpet beater."

"Har har." And giving me little kisses on my cheek like I'm not the boss. Who does she even think she is? Besides my Mary, I mean.

"You really are dirty," she laughed. "Your whole back is wet. Are you my little piggy playing in the mud?"

"You take that back or we aren't friends anymore." I am not a little piggy. Not. I will submit to being compared to a silly goose, whatever a silly goose even looks like or however they act. All the gooses I've ever met have been super serious with the honking and the hissing if you get too close.

"Aww," Mary said without apologizing for implying I'm a little piggy. "C'mon. Inside, into the tub, and then it's dinner time." She steered me toward the back door and stopped on the patio. "Shoes." I got my dirty shoes off. "Socks." I got my dirty socks off. "Shorts, undies, and shirt."

"Har har again, Mary."

"No joking. You're dirty."

"I think I can make it to the laundry room without making a mess." (Fuck yeah main floor laundry! Woohoo!)

"But why risk it?" Smiling like she's having fun at my expense. Nyahh!

"Because we're outside." Like, duh. I'm being hyper, not an exhibitionist.

"It's dark." She folded her arms and tapped her foot. "Need me to undress you," she asked when I gave her the stink eye.

"Ugh, fine." She held out her hand as I turned over the remainder of my apparel like it was contraband. Did I mention it had gotten chilly?

"In you go," Mary said as she held the door open for me. I got past her when she exclaimed, "Hi, Mae!"

"Eep!" Warp speed out of sight I went.

"Hahahaha! Look at you go when you're motivated."

"Not funny!"

"Said princess pouty face."

"Why are you in such a goofy mood all of a sudden?"

"Because my workday is over and I have a pretty little girl to wash."

Well, good reasons, but, "I'm not a little girl!"

"It's even cuter when you say that with the little dirt smudge on your face. Like you played all day with the other littles."

"You … (foot stomp) … urghrrrr! I am not a little!"

"Tots adorbs, Daffy. Bathroom." Nobody even says 'tots adorbs' anymore. "Ah-ah-ah," she said. "Dirty little girls can use the downstairs bath." I made a sharp left into the downstairs bath with Mary hot on my heels. She's always being hot on my something. You think she has the hots for me or something?

She turned on the tap and stopped the drain, then turned and gave me a look I haven't classified yet. She's always coming out with new looks (and the seasons are changing, and she could totally be a model for, like, an Eddie Bauer catalogue). "Um, what," I asked. Probably be worth pausing just to note that I was standing there naked and dirty, and she was standing there clothes and clean, and I was about to get a bath she would be participating in, and none of that was registering as out of the ordinary. Interesting path we've trod to get to this point, but here we are.

"Exactly how much did you spend," she asked.

"Um, well, tax adds nine percent."

"Nine percent of what?"

"Six hundred dollars, give or take," I said as though I had nothing to fear, because I don't. I'm the boss. I can dip into petty cash as needed. I certainly didn't say it sheepishly.

"Six hun…" Ooo, look, flaring nostrils … that's never good. "You … such a naughty girl."

"I'll work it off."

"O yeah, how?"

"Yard work. Ouch!" Such quick hands for someone who works at a computer all day. A little carpal tunnel would be good for my butt.

"I think you just bought yourself a whole lot of doing the dishes."

"What's for dinner?"

"Excuse me! Privileged much?"

"Not privileged! I mean, yes, privileged, but also hungry and something smells good."

"I made lasagna. Can we focus, please?"

"Aww, you made lasagna because it takes a while to cook and now you can take your time giving me a bath cuz you like me and stuff."

"Focus."

"Sorry. Dishes, got it." I am, too, good at focusing! Just … springtime … and nudity … and a hot bath … and I was hungry.

"How much sugar did you have today?"

"Just what was in the gatorade … Six of them. Ya know, I'm outta shape, now that you mention it." She leaned over and shut the water off.

"Lots of dishes, and you're getting your bottom spanked." She sat down on the lid of the toilet, yoinked me over her knee, and rested her hand on my butt, drumming her fingers. "Played in the yard all day, all dirty, over my knee in the bathroom about to get her bare bottom spanked, and then is gonna get a bath. Tell me again you're not a little girl."

"I'm not a little girl! And I'm only over your knee and getting a bath because ..." Dammit.

"Why? Use your words."

"Because you said."

"Mhmm. Because I'm in charge. Know who's not in charge? Little girls."

"But ... I'm a shareholder!" *Hmm.* Awkward pause.

"... Daphne, serious question: did you put something in the gatorade?"

"No ... It makes sense if you listen to the things I don't say." And she so doesn't listen because I've told her that before. I lead a rich inner life with a fast-paced, 30-Rock kinda inner monologue. I'm not random. Other people are just too linear.

"I honestly don't know what to do with you sometimes."

"You have a knack for figuring it out."

"If you're enjoying this, I can take my belt off." Yeah, not so much a fan of the belt. Like, at all.

"No! I mean ... I know I did wrong and I'm ready for my consequence." Been a while since I said that. We got less formal about these things over the years. I mean, when we switched from scenes to lifestyle and, "Ow! OW!! Mary! You're gonna sprain a finger! Warmup! Warmup!"

"It's a punishment, Daphne Ann. You don't get a warmup."

"Eeep!"

"You'd better eep! Six hundred … Did you lose your gosh dang mind this morning or something?" for the record, I'm the one from Wisconsin with the whole Midwest nice stereotype and not once in my entire life have I uttered the phrase *gosh dang*.

"I ordered it on Sunday. OWW!!! Mary, that hurts!"

"It's supposed to hurt, little girl. It's a spanking." O yeah. I forget sometimes. "Are you gonna behave?" SPANK!

"Yes!"

"Good! (SMACK!) Up you get."

I was back on my feet and rubbing my butt before she could change her mind. I felt like I'd gotten away with something. Six hundred bucks (okay, more like seven) when the limit is one hundred? "Um, is that all?"

"Do you need more?"

"No," I meeped.

"Then that's all. In you go." Mary and her directions; up I went and in I got.

"Aich," I exclaimed when my reddened butt made contact with the hot bath water. That's a fun feeling, as is the non-slip texture at the bottom of bathtubs on a freshly spanked butt. Unless she really lets me have it, in which once it would not be fun at all (except in the ways it's still kinda fun).

I reached for the soap expecting and receiving, "I got that," from my Mary.

"I can do it myself," I reminded her.

"Of course you can," Mary said-smirked at me as she took my soap after she sat down on the …

"Where did that come from?"

"What?"

"The stool you're sitting on." *Um, duh?*

"Amazon."

"I mean why'd you buy it."

"Because it hurts my knees giving you a bath kneeling on the floor. Lean forward."

"I'm sorry about the money."

"You can consider four hundred of it a gift."

"Why? Was there something else you were gonna get me? … Asking for my friend."

"Tell your friend no, and remind her how lucky she is she didn't get six hundred dollars' worth of spanking."

"Mary, sometimes I don't you think you listen. See, I got a spanking. My friend didn't." Out of the tub, that would for sure earn me a pop in the butt. In the tub? Heeheeheehee.

"Tell me the truth: so you like getting baths from me?"

"Mhmm." Who wouldn't? Hot water? Check. Mary's soapy hands? Check. Those hands rubbing all over me? Ooo, you better believe that's a check.

"I like giving my little girl baths."

"I'm not a little girl! I'm a noble sovereign being bathed by her handmaid. You are still a maiden, right?"

"Such a little girl. A literary one."

"We can check your maidenhead later." Because I'm nobility I get to decree things like that.

"Do I need to remind you who the domme is, or are you done sassing me?" Because I'm nobility I get to the decree things when Mary lets me.

"Sorry."

"Don't be sorry. Just remember some words are not nice for little girls to say."

"I'm not a little girl." Really!

"Then I guess you don't get your present. Lean back. Time to get your front." Know what's better than slippery, soapy hands on your back? Slippery, soapy hands on your front. Do not doubt. I know things. That's what I do: I spend Mary's money, and I know things (and if that doesn't sound like a shareholder, you ain't hearing from enough shareholders).

Also, "So you did get me something. You fibbed … by omission."

"I got you something when I saw you playing in the yard." She filled a cup I hadn't noticed with water. "If you're gonna be in a kiddie pool, you're gonna have to wear a frilly little girl swimsuit." Close your eyes."

"Marry! That's pbbbbttt (sputter; cough). Urgh!"

"You're supposed to close your mouth when you close your eyes, sweetie." *Sitting on her stool looking so friggin' delighted with herself.* "You're gonna look so cute."

"You didn't!"

"I so did."

"Marrrry!"

"It's just until I take the pictures."

"Pictures!?!"

"No splashing."

"I'm not splashing! I'm pouting!"

"It's not an every time thing. Just when …"

"Just when you wanna mistreat me. Hmmmph!"

"If you're gonna be like that, I'll just hafta send back your other present."

"Go right ahead … Whuddya get me?" Okay, so I like presents. Most of the time.

"A swing," Mary said with that happy-fun tone she uses with our nephew.

"Um," I said all clever like, "you mean like a sex swing?"

Mary's hand stopped what it was doing (washing my hair; *sigh* …) and she leaned over to look me right in the eye. "You are the dirtiest little girl I think I've ever met."

"Maybe that's because I'm. Not. A. Little. Girl!" I'm just a thirty-one-year-old with an overwhelming urge to physically express her love for her wife.

"I got a swing-swing, for the tree. Two, actually. One porch swing to sit in together, and one swing to push you in so you can make cute little squees as you go higher."

"Aww. Thank you. … Um, can we return one?"

"But I wanna sit with you under our tree. Eyes closed." Someone of a more paranoid streak than me might suspect her the rinse was strategically times to shut me up. Luckily, swinging, I've since googled, is good exercise. "Aww, someone looks like a wet puppy. Up you get." Her and her directions. Up I got and out I went.

She dried me off in a towel that's only stayed so fluffy because it's in the downstairs bath and no one showers down there. I couldn't help but notice she was seeming a little amorous, what with the putting her left arm around my belly and right hand grabbing a butt cheek (clarification: mine) and her lips nibbling at my neck as she steered me in front of the mirror.

"Admit it," I said as my knees wobbled. "You're in love with me."

"Every day, Daffy. I think I loved you before I even met you." Oof. Feels. Like the feeling of her lips kissing me all up and down my bare neck. "Will you hold still for me while I comb your pretty red hair?"

I would so do anything for her. Holding still is easy. She reached around me to open the medicine cabinet. "Where'd all this come from?" It's a downstairs bathroom, and we live upstairs. We bathe en suite, like fancy people. We don't keep toiletries in the downstairs bath.

"I thought we agreed we'd use this tub more."

"O yeah. I just forgot you could it's for baths, too." Because I suggested we use it for … drinking wine and playing Battleship. Um, yeah, that's a waterproof game with a nautical theme. And we do have that torpedo in the toy chest …

"Mmm, my silly goose, all sparkly clean. Mwuh!" Heehee! She was being all kissy and lovey-dovey.

"Mary?"

"Yeah, baby?"

"Thanks for taking care of me today."

"I love taking care of you, Daffy." She sighed at me. *Sigh* … She gave me a pop on the butt. Such a fun sensation through a wet towel, which she unwrapped.

"Someone looks cold all of a sudden. I got your jammies in the living room. Go get your diaper basket out and wait for me. She gave me another butt smack before I could get out of butt smacking range. I could feel the adrenaline (and maybe also sugar) of springtime happiness fading now that I was clean and ready for a hot and heavy meal (also, we were having lasagna for dinner teehee!).

I almost forgot to say, "I hate the diapers, Mary," on my way to the living room.

"I know, sweetie, but you'll wear them until you learn," my darling spouse called after me.

"Marrry!" Learn what? That Mary is in charge and I'll wear what she says or else? Because learned it. Top of the class. May not seem that way with my tendency to try to get out of it, but was I not practically skipping down the hall with springtime mirth to do as I was told? After all, I'm a good rule follower.

"Good girl," Mary said to me when she found me on the floor next to the basket and sitting on the blanket she'd presumably put down just for me. "Lay back for me." I did and felt even more tired. Not ready-for-bed tired, but definitely ready-to-be-snuggled tired. And did you hear what my wife called me? Heehee! Not that I'm bragging, but my wife thinks I'm a good girl. *Sigh* …

We went through the motions, and Mary pronounced me pretty as a picture. I don't especially like footie pajamas, but I gotta admit, after a day outside and after a bath and when the temperature drops and the window is open, *shudder* with the fuzzy-warm feelings. I let out another sigh (*sigh* …).

"You gonna make it through dinner before you pass out on me?" O, so she, too, was anticipating me passing out on her? Maybe she meant it another way, but in her lap was my intent.

"Uh-huh," I yawned.

"You were bouncing off the walls a half-hour ago. Such a silly goose."

"Mhmm."

"Daffy …" She sat down next to me and put her arm around my shoulder, and I leaned into her. "How you feeling today with everything? Still okay?"

"Mhmm."

"Anything you wanna talk about? You really doing okay?"

"Yeah. I promise."

"Okay." She kissed my temple. "You just tell me if you need to talk. Anytime." The timer on the oven beeped, and we went to the kitchen where Mary pulled this beautiful lasagna out of the oven. Lasagna is a lot of work, with the prep and layers. Even if it is just for two people. And it looked so yummy!

"Let's let it cool for ten minutes. What salad dressing do you want? … Daffy?" She was only saying that cause I didn't answer her. And because my lip started quivering again. And I don't even know why! Or I did, sorta.

"You made me dinner (sniffle; choke) And you were working all day and you still made dinner (sob; choke; sob)." I'm … not pathetic. It's not pathetic. It's just the little things. The little things, and grief, and being tired. And maybe – just maybe – a sugar crash. Maybe. And grief. For lots of reasons. Grandma was … just the latest reason.

I held out my arms, knowing I could fall forward and Mary would catch me in the tightest, warmest hug. Which she did, cause she loves me and stuff. Really.

Chapter 18: Feelings Are Hard

"You seem a little eager for the real warm weather to get here," Nana said to me.

"What makes you say that," I said knowing exactly what made her say that: my outfit. I had on my one-piece, a pair of shorts, and a pair of old sneakers (ironically not made for sneaking) to work outside in my garden, which Nana very generously offered to help me with. "I just wanna get some sun." Also, my one-piece fetish, but Nana doesn't need to know about that. I mean, seriously, like she needs to know about all our business? She's got enough to try to process, and a girl needs a little mystery in her life.

"You gotta go deeper than that, honey. Here," Nana said and showed me how deep to make a hole for planting my rhododendron.

"You better dig those holes right," my darling spouse said from her position on the veranda (patio) reclined on a throne (chaise lounges from Target) drinking for her golden goblet (cup from some place that gives away souvenir cups; I don't remember where and the dishwasher long ago wore the label off; we are so fucking classy).

"She's doing fine," Nana told her royal pbbbbt!

"She used to hate yard work," Mary said.

"It's different when it's your own yard, and it's not yard work. Sweaty men and paid laborers do yard work. This is gardening." Which is what ladies of leisure such as myself do between juleps on the veranda.

"Wanna tell Nana what happened the last time you complained yard work?"

"No, I do not, and you don't either if you wanna go to bed with someone who likes you tonight," I haughtily replied. Us ladies of leisure are allowed to be haughty. Or so I hoped.

That's when Nana chimed in with, "I could use a cold drink." She pointed a pointed look toward Mary, and I don't think I'd ever seen such a thing, but Mary stood up, said, "I'll make some lemonade," and went inside to do it.

I mean, sure, if I ask for something, she'll do it, but I've thrown Mary plenty of pointed looks. Not so much with the producing of results, much less just declaring a desire and seeing it appear (except sometimes cuz Mary loves me like you wouldn't believe). Pointed looks just seem to tell Mary what to do or say next to get my goat (which is a strange phrase; did someone get their goat got?), and declarations of desires usually end up with me going to do a thing. Which is right and proper given our respective roles. I like getting things for Mary. But it's still fun to see someone else just say something and watch Mary hop to.

"When she comes back, tell her some jewelry would hit the spot," I suggested.

"You guys doing okay?"

"Yeah."

"Just yeah? That's not your usual lovey-dovey answer."

"She's been taking good care of me. I just ... same. Same thing that always bothers me. Am I taking good care of her?"

"I'm sure you are. Besides, didn't you tell me letting her take care of you is how you take care of her?"

"Yeah. Maybe been letting her do that a little too much." Ya know what would be cool? If I could make up my damn mind. "I mean, she's just getting more and more into doting on me, and I don't want it to get out of hand … if it hasn't already." And why would I think that? O why, o why would I think that?

"Do you ever talk about that stuff?"

"Yeah, occasionally." Most often after I've bottled up emotions and let them come pouring outta me in an explosion of misgivings and hurt feelings, at which point Mary paddles me until I'm a hot mess and makes me tell her what's bothering me while reminding me this whole thing coulda been avoided if I had been up front with her in the first place.

Which, yes, but in my defense, feelings are hard! It's not easy talking about this stuff, and it's not easy saying no to Mary when pleasing Mary is, on the whole, the thing I like most. Add in me not working, and it's kinda my whole *raison d'être* right now unless you count consuming my weight in added sugar. Remember balance, as in before the pandemic? A lot of things were out of balance, but a lot of things were in.

And the thing is, I don't know if I wanna go back to school after all. I don't really miss working as much as I did a few months ago, and with Mary's promotion we're really not hurting for the money. Her last raise was pretty much what I'd be making as a first-year teacher (which, holy crap, is a whole 'nother social issues rant to be had, but it can wait). But I can't keep living like this! Another year, and I'll be in diapers 24/7 because that's what you do with people who have taken leave of their senses and live in rubber rooms. And I look fat in a straitjacket (true story).

"Maybe," Nana logically suggested, "you should have a talk with Mary."

"Yeah. I know," I said as I placed my plant in the hole. What is dirt made of anyway?

"I'm sorry."

"For what?"

"For bringing up a touchy subject."

"It's not touchy. It's just … sensitive."

"Let's talk about something else. Did you get an appointment for a vaccine yet?"

"Nope, and let's not talk about that because I'm just gonna scream at the sky if we go down that road."

"Poor thing. You really are having a rough few weeks. Wanna come over tomorrow and do something fun?"

"Yeah. I'd like that."

"Lemonade," Mary said from the patio. "I made it fresh from a powdered mix."

"Took you long enough," I said because bratting is more fun that serious conversations.

"Daphne Ann, you are gonna bite off more than you chew today. I smell a spanking coming."

"Marrry, don't say stuff like that in front of Nana," I stood up and dusted myself off.

"I was thinking the same thing with a sass mouth like that," Nana said before dusting me off some more.

"I am so overparented," I grumbled. Like there was any way the day wouldn't end with Mary wanting to give me a bath and put one of those stupid diapers on me. Yes, I like being bathed, but a little moderation keeps things interesting, mainly by stopping them from getting boring, and Mary had definitely been going the route of using bath time to dress me in cutesy little girl things for the evening (or entire day). Remember the punishment panties? I need to bring those back into my life (and fuck my life since that's what it's come to).

But nope, no way am I on a collision course with an emotional catastrofuck that ends with me bawling over Mary's knee. Nope. No way ... Really. Please?

Chapter 19: A-Hiking We Will Go

Just because I'm the bottom doesn't mean misbehavior is exclusively my domain. Mary is more adventurous than me. If I had my way, I never would have, say, gotten my panties taken down in a Macy's dressing room and paddled in full hearing of who the heck knows. That's courting some serious consequences (like court), and it's partly just luck that we've never gotten caught. At first, Mary would tell me that once she explained my transgression to the whomever, they'd just tell her she was right to spank me and to not wait until we got home, but of course that was just her being a smartmouth. At a certain point, and we're aware of this, we're gonna hafta stop playing like that in public.

But not yet! And also, some of those (most of them) were not play. They were me getting my bottoms dropped in public and getting spanked like a person who earned a spanking (which I usually had). So for now at least, we can still play in public places, and Mary being Mary (i.e. always having to be in control) decided that's what we'd do with our Sunday without, ya know, telling me.

We hiked all over creation, or so it seemed to me. If we walked any further, we wouldn't be in the same park anymore. Mary declared "This is the spot," and we sat down to eat our backpack-temperature lunch. Growing up, Mom thought I was too skinny and obsessed over me not eating lunch at school sometimes. Back and forth we went on it until I explained that as much as I loved her, her Healthy Choice turkey on white bread with Miracle Whip was even more tasteless after it had been in my locker all morning. I was, like, fourteen before I found out about real mayonnaise, which is ironic given I grew up in Wisconsin with ranch dressing everything.

"Thanks for packing lunch," Mary said to me as we set our meagre feast before us on our picnic blanket.

"You're welcome. Thanks for getting me out of the house ... We should go camping."

"I thought you didn't like it."

"I don't like being stuck in our house even more, and I could give it another shot. It would be better this time of year. We shouldn't have gone in the summer."

"You didn't mind the skinny dipping part," my predator of a wife reminisced while being all smiley and eating a strawberry. Pretty woman eating strawberries ... *subby drool noises.*

"That's something we should do – plan our next adventure for when the pandemic is over. Where are we going," I asked.

"Where do you wanna go?"

"I asked first."

"What if we went to Europe again?"

"Which part?"

"Maybe do a few countries. I could take a couple weeks off, and we could see a few places. Eat too much gelato. Drink all the wine."

"I think we should go back to Germany."

"Why there?"

"Dirndls."

Mary rolled her eyes at me in a nice way. "You have the cutest fetishes."

"I'm just the bodice ripping type. How's the hummus," I ask while sliding my foot toward hers for some footsie.

"It's good. What if we did a whole alpine thing? We could start in Germany and go to Austria, Switzerland, and Italy?"

We planned our trip in our heads, and lord know when we'll get to take it. Hopefully a year from now, though maybe sooner. I wouldn't mind taking an alpine trip in the winter. There are so many mountains I haven't slid down on my ass shouting for the other skiers to get out of the way. It's not that I'm not athletic. It's just that I'm not so much with the coordination on slippery surfaces. Surely I'm not the only lesbian who gets discombobulated when confronted with a slipper surface. This one time in college …

Anyhoo, I bet it would be just as fun to toboggan. I'm good at that. I grew up in Wisconsin after all. I even know how to ice fish. What you do, see, is dress in layers and drink schnapps in an ice shack. You may even catch a fish if you remember to put your line in the water.

We finished our lunch, put our things away, made out like freshmen, and just when I thought we were going to fold up the blanket, Mary said to me, "Hold on."

"Why?" I was kinda eager to get back and we had a long walk ahead of us.

"Before we go, I wanna deal with your attitude."

"What attitude," I asked with a boatload of attitude.

"On the way here you asked, 'how much further.' I think we should just nip that kind of bad attitude in the butt."

"It's 'bud' and I wasn't complaining. I was just asking."

"And now we have this whole other problem to deal with," she said with her I-can-keep-doing-this-for-as-long-as-I-want smile plastered to her face.

"You're just making stuff up! … And what other problem?"

"You're not over my lap yet."

"But …"

"Exactly – your butt isn't over my lap."

"But people."

"We didn't see anybody in the last two miles before we got here, and don't you wanna be my submissive little girl?"

"Well, yes to the submissive and girl parts."

"You just love girl parts so much."

"But couldn't we wait until we get home?"

"But Daffy," Mary said with her snarky smile plastered on, "don't you want to be by submissive little girl?"

"You said that already … and yes, but …" Stupid feelings making me feel feelings with the conflicted feelings and things and stuff. "Fine," I said and scooted over to her. Why do I always give in (also known as *submitting*) just because I'm the submissive?

"The last time we did this, it was your idea, if memory serves," Mary reminded me. "Over my lap."

"But that was further from the trail, and there was more stuff between us and it."

She flipped up my skirt anyway. "And as a concession to that fact, I'll leave your undies on."

"Mary, no! Eeeep!" *Buh-huh! Urghh! Fnnrmrmrrr.*

"Why you eepin'?" She was swirling her fingertips around on my butt cheeks, and yes, I liked it, but eeeeeep!

"Because you're so mean to me." Letting me keep my panties on was not so much an ideal situation because wedgie. Not an atomic wedgie, but maybe a napalm wedgie because it burned with the panties practically splitting me in two.

"I'm not mean, Daffy. I'm strict, because little girls need someone in their life to keep them on the straight and narrow."

"Nothing you've ever done to me has kept me straight," I snarked with all the snark I could snark to prove she's not nearly so good at snark as I am when I'm snarking. There was world weariness in my snark, too.

"And thank goodness for that."

"And I'm not a little girl." Really.

"O, so it's a big girl laying across my lap about to get her bare bottom spanked."

"Yes, and there are no contradictions in that sentence whatsoever, so just do what you wanna – hhhhh! – Mary! We're in public!" With those fingers of her going places and doing things. That'll teach me to give her blanket permission to do what she wants with me. Lesson noted and learned.

"Now that you say that, this place does look a lot different from our house. But back to business. Why are you getting your bare bottom spanked?"

"Because you said.

"I think there's a little more reason to it than that."

"Because you made up a reason and then you said." Minor risk, but I felt compelled to tell the truth. What's the worst she could do? Spank me?

She chuckled instead. "Sounds about right. Now, it's okay if you need to struggle and make adorable little subby noises during your spanking. That's normal for a little girl getting her bare butt warmed, and I won't have any trouble controlling your body. I've given lots of little girls spankings."

"You've given the same *grown woman* lots of spankings lately."

"That's the kind of attitude we need to adjust," Mary said, raising her hand.

"Injustice brings out my attitude," I managed to say just before her hand made contact with my butt. "Ow! Marrrry, go easy on me. I'm tiny."

"Pshaw. You are not (SMACK). In fact, you're a larger-than-life figure (SMACK!)." SMACK SMACK SMACK!!! "There, that should remind you who's boss."

"I never forgot ... And is that all?"

"For now."

"Um, but ... hmmph! ... You're so mean sometimes." Gets me all wound up and just gives me love pats. Creates a whole nether regions situation and just leaves me to deal while she delights in watching me squirm. Damn but I love her and stuff. Wonder what it's like to be normal? Probably must be horrible.

"But I'm so nice the rest of the time."

"Are you just gonna sit there, or are you gonna kiss me and stuff." I rolled off her lap and tried to affect my kinky minx pose. Know what destroys a kinky minx pose? Picking a wedgie. So my attempt came off more as my my-underwear-is-virtually-inside-my-butt pose.

She scortled. "You were so shy a moment ago."

"Stop living in the past, Mary." But in the present, still with the wedgie. Like ... ow.

"My little hedonist," Mary said before pouncing on me like a she-wolf. That's what she is, ya know, a she-wolf, whereas I am just a (lusty) bunny trying to make my way through the big bad woods without getting eaten.

But I'd have to save getting eaten until we returned to the suburbs. I settled for getting kissed and petted, and now that I think on it, if Mary and me were a YouTube video, it would be one of those predator-loves-prey videos where people ooo and aww when a German shepherd takes care of a rabbit or goose (and everybody would call me a silly goose, which I am not – really!).

But that's not what we got caught doing. "You have a leaf in your hair," I said to Mary when we were done fooling around.

"You have a beautiful smile," she said back and made me all snurfy and smol feeling and happy.

"You like me," I said with my derpy-smile on. Mary gets to be beautiful and poised, and I get to be all flustered and derpy.

"Of course I do. That's why I'm so mean to you." She took a deep breath and sighed. "So let's get your underpants on and we can go."

"They're already on," I pointed out, and they'd even worked themselves free. Well, one side (yay progress!).

"Those are not age appropriate."

"Well, duh! You picked them out … Stupid kittens." Smiling at me from my panties like they're right at home with another pus … anyhoo …

"And besides," Mary continued without acknowledging my protest because she loves continuing without acknowledging my protest, "You couldn't even keep them clean."

"I did too! You're just …"

"Mean. I know. And if they're so clean, why don't you peel them off and give them a sniff."

"Ewww! We've been hiking and … And you put 'em there."

"Stop living in the past, Daffy," she winked.

"Don't you wink at me with your throwing my words back at me from like fifteen minutes ago." That's nine hundred whole seconds!

She crawled over to me on fours (cuz she's a she-wolf) and kissed me on the cheek and then (such effrontery) tapped me on the nose and said, "You're pretty when you're pouty and flustered." And then she kissed me again. "Stand up."

"Flattery will get you nowhere," I said as I stood up. I really need to have a word with my brain about doing what I say and not just what Mary says.

"Did I mention you're a very good girl today?" Also, flattery has gotten Mary all the places and most of the things (okay, all the things, if I'm being honest).

"Marrry, why you gotta go pushing all my buttons?"

"Because we haven't gone anywhere in a while, and I wanna make the very most of it." She took a deep breath and sighed. "And because I like getting you hot and bothered and watching you squirm, and I know you like it, too."

"Do not." Except yep (mostly).

"I think your real fetish is playing hard to get. Just barely hard to get," she added with a chuckle.

"I am, too, hard to get!"

"And your other fetish is just being oppositional."

"It's called bratting, Mary … And I'm not a brat."
Really!

"Ya know what else I think?"

"If I ask you and say please with extra sprinkles with a cherry on top will you tell me," I said. A hint of sarcasm may have crept into my voice.

"I think when get home you're gonna need to be paddled hard."

"But … Yes'm."

"Or we can do it on the way home at the rest stop."

"Home is good," I meeped. I love our home. Paddled at home sounds wonderful.

"If we have that resolved, gimme your feetsies."

I grumbled as I complied. "Why are you taking my shoes off? Ya gonna give me a piggyback ride all the way to the car?"

"I'm gonna put you in a goodnite so you don't piddle on the trail on the way back."

"O. Better than a diaper I guess."

"We'll save the diaper for the car."

"But I don't need it for the car … Or anywhere!" Nor a Goodnite to not piddle on the trail! Really!

"I'll make a deal with you," she said as she got my shoes off. "If you can keep your pullup dry all the way back to the car, you can wear it home. Won't that be fun?"

"Sublırumuhmınınder ressefraiter."

"What?"

"I was grumbling!"

"Lay back." Which I did, and Mary reached up under my skirt and took my panties down. "Bet it feels good to have these yucky underoos off."

"They felt fine until you pulled them up to my brain."

"And now I'll pulled them down to your ankles. The universe balances. Lift those hips."

This is the part where I blacked out. Or wish I had. But things did go black for a minute. I was lifting my hips and all of a sudden, Mary's eyes got big and she threw the blanket over me, or the half of the blanket I wasn't laying on.

"Hi," Mary said to … someone.

"Hi," someone said back. "Good day for it."

O my god, make your inane small talk walking and fast.

"Yep."

"So …"

"Well, nice chatting with you."

Go the fuck away!

"Bye."

What's happening?

"They're leaving," Mary whispered.

"Can I come out?"

"Wait until they're around the bend … okay, quick."

Mary ninjaed me. There was a blinding light, and when it went away, I was wearing a goodnite. How does she do that? It's not nice to keep secrets from your wife, and, darn it, I wanna be a ninja too.

I got a very quick hug, and Mary ninjaed our stuff into the pack while I got my shoes on. We hiked pretty damn fast in the direction of the Subaru with Mary looking behind us every few minutes.

"I think we're okay, Mary." Like, the person wasn't creepy so far as I could tell. They wanted to chat, but it didn't seem dangerous (at least not from under the blanket).

"Quicker, Daff."

"You're scaring me. What's wrong?"

"Nothing. Let's just get out of here."

It took us two hours to walk there, and we did the return trip in less than an hour and a half. We encountered other people, and if Mary was feeling unsafe, she didn't say anything to them or seem to feel less unsafe because we weren't alone. I couldn't get a word out of her other than, "We'll talk about it at the car."

So when we did get to the car, we were soaked with sweat (and bear in mind, I don't sweat; I glisten; but I was soaked with sweat), a little out of breath, and tired. We dumped our stuff in the back, where we had also put a cooler with some cold drinks for when we got back because Mary still won't go in a store to get stuff.

I sat down on our tailgate and quaffed by Gatorade. Much of said Gatorade ended up on my shirt when Mary threw her arms around me like, well, the way I throw my arms around her (but her arms are bigger than mine).

"Mary, what's wrong?"

"I'm so sorry (sniff). Are you okay?"

"Yeah." I gave her a kiss on her hair. "Don't get all teary. I'm fine."

"That was my fault."

"We pressed our luck once too often."

"But you didn't even want to."

"I didn't red light either."

"I'm supposed to keep you safe."

"I am safe." I kissed her again. "We're both fine."

She took a big sniff and kissed me. "When we get home, I'm giving you a bath and putting you in your jammies."

"You are such a silly goose," I told her. "Want me to drive?"

"No. I'm fine."

"Can we stop and get ice cream."

"Ha. Drive through."

"See, you do take good care of me."

"I love you so much."

"I love you, too."

Chapter 20: Ewwww!

Mary was so on my shit list today. I mean, how was I the one in trouble? I was the wronged party! She … urgh! Dammit! I was not a happy camper.

"Mary, please," I asked for the bajillionth time.

"Sorry, Daff, I just can't see what's bothering you so much."

"You can too!"

"Why don't you go play outside?"

And you better believe I stomped every step of the way outside.

So what happened? Well, as usual, it began with Mary and her wandering hands.

"Hey," I exclaimed very politely, "what are you doing?" Very politely considering she just goosed me.

"Checking to see if you're still dry."

"Of course I am! I'm wearing panties."

"You don't need to be embarrassed. Lots of little girls have accidents."

"I'm not a little girl. And what is with you lately?" She's being all handsy and cranking up the kink. She's like a full blown big with the teasing and the hands and did I mention I'm not a little cuz guess the frick what? I AM NOT A LITTLE! REALLY!!! Hmmph.

"I'm just trying to take good care of you."

"O my god, Mary, just o my god. You are seriously channeling my mother with that line … It's not funny," I said so out of patience with her and her chuckling.

"Aww, c'mere and let me make it better."

"No," I said and folded my arms and stayed right where I was on the couch.

"Are you grumpy 'cause you need the potty?"

I accidentally let out an exasperated chuckle. Those can mean lots of things, but the chief one is being exasperated. "Mary…"

"Okay, okay. C'mon, let's go." She took my hand and gently pulled me off the couch.

"Where are you taking me," I asked with all the weariness I carry on behalf of mankind (and you're welcome, btw, not that any thanks are necessary; just send money and jewels).

To fast forward, because this is not the main point in my retelling of this episode of mistreatment, I ended up getting diapered on our bed. I didn't take it laying down either. Or I did literally, but figuratively I hmmmphed and kicked my heels and grunted and verbalized my frustration until Mary gave me one heck of a spank on my thigh. I hope it hurt her hand at least as much as it hurt me. "Do you need more," she asked me, "or are you gonna be a good girl and let me get your diaper on you?"

I just crossed my arms and held still. It's super not fair that she's strong enough to lift my ankles. There's just no way to fight that. Not that I would because I am a good girl, but I managed to mumble, "It's your diaper."

"Yeah yeah," Mary said like she'd heard that before because she has, "and you're just using it for me."

"Exactly."

At least she let me put my shorts back on. Or so I thought. Fast forward a few hours more.

"Um, Mary," I said nervously.

"Mhmm," she replied.

"Um, nothing," I said because I chickened out.

So another hour passed, and I said, "Um, Mary?"

"Mhmm," she replied.

"Um, I could, um, I need … I'm wet."

"Hmm," she said and turned back to her tablet.

"Well, um, are you …" And I stopped because the answer was clear now with the way she rolled over to her other shoulder to read her whatever she was reading.

And another hour passed. "Mary, I need a change." I was droopy. Or I was upright and my … (nope!) Mary's garment was droopy.

"I don't think you do," Mary said like she's innocent of anything at all which she isn't which is why she's on my list. Urgh!!!

"My shorts are gonna get wet," I didn't whine because I don't do that but also, I did that. "Can I please change?"

"I can't tell if you're wet, so you must be dry."

"What are you even talking about." She could damn well tell. Everybody could damn well tell, or they could have if they were there to do the damn telling.

"I'd check you myself, but the last time I did that you got very cross with me."

O, come the fuck on. "Marrrry, this is uncomfortable. And I'm telling you it needs changed."

"And who would trust a pampers piddler to know when they need fresh huggies?" She had that spark in her eye she always gets when she's having so much fun teasing me. It's very attractive, which is great and all but also, urgh!

"Mary! I want out NOW!"

"Is raising your voice at me ever a good idea," Mary asked me. Ya know what she has? A Socratic lecturing fetish. My mind flashed back to this time involving a bar of soap and a cane.

"No," I meeped. "Sorry, but, Mary, please?"

"Why don't you go play outside?"

And now you're all caught up. I stomped outside not because Mary told me to but because I was good and peeved, and I needed some space (also because Mary told me to). I get that she was teaching me a lesson. I'm not exactly sure, but I think the lesson is don't object to Mary touching my panties to – quote – checked for wetness – unquote. Anyone who thinks being a lifestyle submissive is easy doesn't know what the hell they're talking about. I signed on to certain things, and I like the things, but sometimes Mary and me get out of sync with the things. Sometimes I want more than she does, and sometimes she wants more than me, and that means we both get put upon a bit.

The difference is I get too bratty or clingy when I'm the one who wants more whereas Mary gets too handsy and quick to goose and quick to spank and just too much with the teasing. These little swings occupy this weird space. I don't know how long it will last (usually not more than a day) so it's never clear if it's worth directly saying something or indirectly saying something or just letting it go.

Nature decided for me. I mean, sure, I could have let nature take its course with me doing nothing to stop it or change the outcome, but I like those shorts. Besides which, I heard Nana in her garden, and I know if I lingered

much longer she'd hear me and find me in that …
condition. I had no choice but to tug up my big girl pants
and confront Mary.

Now, confrontation can take many forms, and
you're probably thinking it would take a confrontational
form as that's a common thing to have happen when
you're confronting someone. My confrontation was less
confrontational and more serving up my pride on a platter.
So maybe less confrontation than manipulation, but as a
submissive, ya gotta keep that tool in the toolbox. Besides,
I knew Mary would like it.

I went back inside and found Mary, who was
getting something prepped for dinner.

"I thought I told you to play outside," she said with
that spark sparking. "Do you need a spanking to do what
you're told today?"

"I need to go potty."

"Honey, that's what your diapee is for."

Cue crocodile tears. "But it'll leak and I'll make a
puddle and you'll be mad at me and I wanna be a good
girl for you." I'd add the *boohoos*, but I'm sure you can
imagine. I shuffled (not waddled, I'll have you and the
whole damn world know) to Mary so I could bury my face
in her chest and elicit all the pity.

I got within six inches when she reached out and
put her hand on my chest. "Did I arrive in town on a turnip
truck today to make you think you could try crocodile
tears with me?"

Dammit! Hmmph. "Mary, you're gonna make me
cry for real if you don't lemme change. This is gross and
I want out and I want you to be nice to me today." Her
face softened. "Please let me out," I didn't whimper.

She sighed and made her I-can-never-say-no-to-that-face face. "Like I can say no to that face." See? "Let get you in a dry diapee."

She held my hand all the way up the stairs while I tried, "Can I wear panties?"

"Of course not, pumpkin belly."

"Can I go to the bathroom first?"

"Silly goose, that's what your diapees are for."

"Can I wear pullups?"

"With the puddle you made in that diapee? Absolutely not."

"Well, do I get to pick anything today?"

"Of course you do," she said as we entered our bedroom "You can pick out the kind of diaper you want to wear."

"'Want' to wear," I grumped, which she ignored.

"And what kind of cookies we bake tonight."

"This Saturday is more fun for you than me," I said bluntly.

"Would it make you feel better if I let you eat cookies until you get a belly ache and then rubbed your tummy?"

" … Yes."

"Deal. Which diaper do you want?"

"I'll accept the bunny ones." It is almost Easter after all.

"Goodness, you are soaked. I wish you'd said something," Mary snarked while wiping me down.

"Har har … Mary?"

"Yeah, baby?" Why was she so happy changing that diaper? She just looked so … happy, with the smiling smile and smiling eyes.

"Could we …" I was going to ask if she could cool it with the potty stuff, but that smile. And I am eager to please. I chickened out. "… watch a movie tonight?"

Because things always work out when I don't talk about them until them the feelings spill over. Um, really.

"Of course we can. Lift your hips for me." I guess when she was situating her diaper under me she saw my face. "Hey, what's wrong, Daffy?"

"Nothing."

"Yes there is."

"I just … need you to read my signals a little better today." She frowned, sealed the diaper on me, and laid down next to me.

She kissed me on the shoulder before saying, "I'm sorry, honey. I just got caught up."

"It's okay."

"No, it's not. Are you okay?"

"Mhmm."

"Do you wanna change back into undies?"

"Not if this makes you happy."

"Does it make you happy?"

I had to bite down on my lip. "You make me happy."

"You're such a brave good girl for speaking up. I'll do better."

"I know. You always do."

"Is it alright if I call you *bunny butt* tonight?"

"I am not a bunny butt," I giggled. Though we do have that costume from that one party in the basement…

"I like the idea of you being my bunny."

"Why a bunny?"

"Cute and soft and snuggly."

"You've never had a real bunny, have you?" They are not snuggly. They are claw-wielding bastards sons of the dirt (I had a bad experience once).

"I don't want the real thing. I want you. What can I do to make you feel better?"

"Can we do the cookie thing?"

She scortled. "We can do the cookie thing. You gonna be my clingy shadow for the rest of the day?"

"Yes please."

She smooched me on the neck from where she was behind me, being the big spoon. "Good."

"And can we turn the air conditioning way up and put on our fuzzy pajamas?"

"Hehe. We can, and maybe we can find you some bunny jammies online."

"You don't gotta buy me anything. I forgive you."

"I don't gotta buy you anything, but I wanna see you in bunny jammies, and do you know why?"

"Why?"

"Because they don't make silly goose jammies." She pinched my side where I'm ticklish.

"Marrry! Heehee!"

"You're my good girl."   OMG, my wife thinks I'm a good girl. All the feels.

"And you're my Mary."

Sigh…

Chapter 21: Okay, So I have One Vice

Mary and I haven't exactly gotten along today, and that's never what you want on Easter. The problem is that I am indisputably right, and I wish Mary would stop disputing me. It began between the shower and zoom church, when Mary got an Easter "outfit" ready for me.

"Mary, I'd rather not," I said very politely. I'm very polite, in case you haven't noticed (and shame on you because I'm told I'm very noticeable in a look-at-that-dork way).

"O, c'mon. It has a bunny on it. Just lay down."

"I just wanna wear regular clothes today."

"But I got it just for you to wear on Easter," she claimed. Dubiously claimed, I might add, because I'd worn one of those diapers before. "You're gonna hurt my feelings if you don't wear it."

"See," I countered, "that's just one of those things you say to make me eager to please." As if I'm not already the eager-to-please type.

"That could be, Daffy, but do you really wanna risk it?"

So I ended up wearing a bunny diaper all day (and no, it's not made outta real bunnies, ya buncha smartasses who don't even smartass as good as me), and it was a pretty good day up until our current drama. I got caught doing something I shouldn't have been doing, and Mary for some reason got very dramatic about it.

"I won't do this, Daphne. I won't stand around here and watch it happen. I can't do it again."

"I only had two!"

"That's how it starts, Daphne. That's always how it starts."

"This is so not worth issuing ultimatums over, Mary. It's not a big deal."

"It is a big deal. I love you too much to just watch you get all hyper and get in trouble and then spend all evening with a tummy ache."

"Well, that was my last one."

"Do not lie to me, Daphne Ann. Do. Not. Lie. I want them all. Every last peanut butter egg, or so help me I will make you eat each one while I bathbrush your butt to oblivion."

"Urgh!" I started to walk away.

"Where are you going?"

"To get the list."

"What list?"

"Of where I hid them."

"You made a list of where you hid them? You got so many you had to make a list?"

"Ya can't put all your eggs in one basket, Mary." Geez – everybody knows that.

Assholes! Assholes assholes assholes! And butt faces.

I went inside, washed my hands, dried my hands, and threw the dish towel back on the counter because I am fierce. Or just pissed off. And to compound my crappy morning, I knocked a glass on the floor. Mary almost instantly appeared.

"You okay? What happened," she asked me.

"I'm fine. I knocked a glass off the counter." She walked over to me and, not kidding, picked me up. "Mary!"

"You're wearing sandals," she said and deposited me on the kitchen table. "You'll get cut." Which I most very probably and perhaps definitely wouldn't.

"I can clean it up," I reminded her.

"I got it. What happened?"

"I tossed the towel on the counter and knocked the glass off. Sorry."

"Accidents happen." She got the broom out.

"They ate my flowers."

"What flowers?"

"All the bulbs I planted. Look outside." She stopped what she was doing and tiptoed to the back door.

"I'm sorry, Daffy," she said when she looked outside and saw that every single flower from every single bulb I'd planted was gone. That's one hundred and thirty-five tulips and crocuses and snowdrops, and some asshole of a deer or rabbit or something ate every last one. Every. Last. Damn. One. Fucker!

"I worked hard on those." Sort of. I dug tiny holes, put the bulb in, and covered them. I guess that's kinda not so hard, but not the point. Maybe I emotionally invested a little too much in flowers, but I needed the colors. Reds and yellows and purple and blues and pinks. I needed to see color in my spring after twelve months of immunocompromised quarantine. "There won't be more flowers blooming in our yard for weeks now."

"We can buy some tulips. I'll even plant them with you."

"Thank you," I sighed, "but it's not the same. I made those ones." Well, not really, but planting from a seed or a bulb is so much more rewarding than planting a plant.

Mary resumed her sweeping while I vented and called down the coyotes and hawks to take care of whatever ate my flowers. The bystanders can go about their business, but the ones who did the chewing are on my list of things to subject to the withering power of nature via the power of wishful thinking. Another year of quarantine, and I'll probably be one of those insufferable people who talk about manifesting their desires.

"And we need chicken wire and some spray stuff to keep them away," I said aloud to add to my mental shopping list.

"And I'll hire a neighborhood kid to sit out there all night with a flashlight and an air horn," Mary offered.

Which was sweet of her, but, "I'm serious, Mary. All my flowers." A little bit of whining, which you all know I never do (really!) crept in there.

"I know, sweetie." I did some world class pouting while she finished cleaning up my mess (except I don't ever pout, so technically I didn't. It was more mourning, I guess).

"Come on," Mary said when she put the broom away.

"Thank you for cleaning up after me."

"You're welcome."

"Where are we going?"

"Bed."

"O, sympathy sex," I said. Maybe I'd be more excited for it by the time we got up the stairs. It's not that I have a high libido but that fifteen seconds is a long time, more than enough for me to get in the mood.

When we got to our bedroom, Mary sat down, bent over and took my sandals offs, then popped the button on my shorts. "Why am I getting a spanking," I asked. Which may have been a leap of logic, but her sitting on the bed with me in front of her while she pops the button on my shorts, well, ya might say it conjures memories.

She gave me a quick kiss on my tummy. "You're not, you silly goose."

"I'm not a silly goose. I'm just someone who's had their shorts taken down for many, many spankings." She stood up and turned the covers down. "Hop in." I made a goofy grin at her that was my best attempt to be alluring and sexy and slid in. I wouldn't so much mind Mary getting in with me clothed and having me fumble around under the sheets trying to gain entry to her pants. Or her clothes staying on while she used her teeth to … Anyhoo …

Yet I couldn't help but notice I was also still wearing panties and my tee, and for someone who was going to be getting in bed with me, Mary was suspiciously tucking me in and giving me a kiss on the forehead. Not that I was so in the mood as to be counting on shenanigans, but huh?

"What are you doing," I asked as she gave me a head pat.

"Putting you down for a nap."

"But I don't wanna take a nap."

"You'll feel better after a little sleep. I'll come get you in a bit."

And then she left. Like, what the fuck? 'Feel better?' I felt fine. I was miffed about my flowers (okay, pissed), but I didn't need or want a nap. Mary could've, ya know, asked me.

I got out of bed, put on some pandemic chic no-button shorts, and went back downstairs. I don't know where Mary went, but I went to the kitchen to get a glass of water. For my trouble, I collected both a glass of water and a spank on my butt.

"What are you doing out of bed?"

"I didn't want a nap, but I did want a glass of water. What are you up to?"

"Putting you back down for your nap."

For someone whose wife didn't want to take a nap, Mary sure was taking me back upstairs for a nap. What was this? Was this Mary, as she had been lately, pioneering her own path on the ageplay stuff? Because I distinctly remember asking her to slow that down. I even have a diary entry literally spelling that out.

"I don't want a nap, Mary."

"But you'll feel better after you take one." She's awfully handsy sometimes, a delightful quality when I want her to be and something not so delightful when I don't especially when her to be and downright annoying when I downright don't want her to be. Well, I didn't just then want her to be.

"But I'm not tired."

"Then just rest your eyes. In you go," she said as she stood next to the bed again.

"Marrrry."

"Daffy, in you go."

"But whyyyy?"

"Because I said so. Unless you don't want to go to sleep because you're afraid to close your eyes without a diapee on. Is that the problem?"

"Marrrrrry! But … urgh!"

"In," she said as she guided me onto the mattress and gave me another smack on my butt. "And stay in until I come get you. If I find you out of bed, I'm going to spank." *O yeah, who?*

And with that the friggin' dictatress turned, strode across the room, and closed the door behind her. For once in my life (really!), my frustration got the better of me and I threw a pillow at the door. Like, seriously, how the fuck was I back in bed?

To say I was displeased would be an understatement. We had just talked about her being all big without me wanting her to be. Yes, we all sometimes get into our headspace and push the envelope, and sometimes that leads to new fun we didn't know we liked. And yes, sometimes we deliberately try new things to see how they go, like, o, the very first time she made me wear a pullup, and holy schnikees what a mixed bag that's been. And yes, as a submissive I like her to be in charge and make decisions, but only if she's reading my signals. And didn't I say like a week ago to take two steps back?

Bigging out is a new term I'm using. It's like wigging out except it's when someone gets all into their big space and makes you do little stuff even when you're not in your little headspace, which I'm not ever in because I AM NOT A LITTLE! I've said so a bunch of times.

I like it when Mary pushes the envelope, but only when I'm in the mood. Some other day she wants to put me down for a nap, fine. That day, I was not in the mood even for twenty minutes or however long she was going to make me stay there.

I got out of bed and crept out of the room when I suddenly remembered I don't ever have to creep anywhere. If I didn't want to take a nap, I didn't have to. That's called being an adult and an agent of my own destiny and a master of my own fate. It's called a lot of other things, too. If Mary had a problem with it, I'd just tell her how I felt, like an adult.

I got all the way to the landing on the stairs when I spotted Mary, who turned like predator or a terminator and spotted me from the bottom of the stairs.

"I'm …"

And that's as far as I got when Mary said, "What did I say would happen if you got out of bed before I came to get you?"

And she's on her way up the stairs. "Mary, I don't want to take a nap. Could you just please…"

"No, I cannot just please. When Momma says …"

Excuse me? When who says?

"Mary! Red light."

There's More Mary and Daphne!

Daphne and Mary have a lot of adventures ahead of them as their marriage, kink, and lives continue to evolve, and Daphne tries to avoid becoming the little girl Mary sees her as.

There are five – count 'em! – five more volumes of *I'm Not A Little Girl*, including one more sequel to this volume that will be released in Spring and Summer 2021.

Chapters in-progress will be posted to Patreon before a final round of revision and will then make their way into the next volume for Kindle and paperback.

Check back on Amazon for the next volume, or head to patreon.com/alex_bridges.

Check out Alex's Books on Amazon and Patreon!

Alex's Other Books and Stories

You can find Alex's fiction on Patreon and SubscribeStar, which is updated multiple times a week and currently contains over 100 pieces of content, including work–in–progress drafts of the remaining chapters of *I'm Not a Little Girl*, femdom/ABDL series *Raising Husbands,* and short stories in spanking, ageplay, feminization and ABDL. Some stories are also in audio format and narrated by a professional disciplinarian and content creator. Instant access to all chapters and stories for just a few dollars a month.

I'm Not a Little Girl (Really!) Vol. 1

Meet 36-year-old Mary and 30-year-old Daphne, deeply in love and stuck in the cutest and kinkiest newlywed phase ever.

Once upon a time, our hero and narrator, Daphne, told her then-girlfriend Mary that she wanted their domestic discipline fetish to be their lifestyle. Fast forward to married life, and Daphne finds herself subject to strict and loving discipline from her doting wife even Daphne's best bambi eyes can't get her out of.

Over the years, what began as a spanking relationship has taken on more of an ageplay flavor, and Mary is about to introduce a new element sure to tickle their (and your) erotic humiliation, lezdom, spanking, and ageplay tickle spots. Daphne is nothing if not a good little rule follower (most of the time), but she insists she is not a little girl even as the hairbrush comes out and the shorts go down.

It helps that Daphne is madly in love with her wife and wants nothing so much as her approval, and of course Mary loves her Daphne and wants nothing so much as to see her safe and happy.

Theirs is a one-of-a-kind romance sure to make you jealous (and excited).

NSFW. Contains spanking, erotic humiliation, ageplay, ABDL, exhibitionism, lezdom, and consensual non-con. For readers 18+ only. All characters are 18+.

I'm Not a Little Girl (Really!) Vol. 2

Volume 2 in this series of romance novels continues the love story of Mary and Daphne right where Volume 1 left off, following 36-year-old Mary and 30-year-old Daphne, deeply in love and stuck in the cutest and kinkiest newlywed phase ever.

Once upon a time, our hero and narrator, Daphne, told her then-girlfriend Mary that she wanted their domestic discipline fetish to be their lifestyle. Fast forward to married life, and

Daphne finds herself subject to strict and loving discipline from her doting wife that even Daphne's best bambi eyes can't get her out of.

Their drift from domestic discipline to ageplay continues as Mary leans into the new attire for Daphne sure to tickle their (and your) erotic humiliation, lezdom, spanking, and ageplay tickle spots. Daphne does her best to be Mary's good girl, but it gets harder when the COVID-19 pandemic strikes and they quarantine in their home indefinitely.

It helps that Daphne is madly in love with her wife and wants nothing so much as her approval, and of course Mary loves her Daphne and wants nothing so much as to see her safe and happy.

Theirs is a one-of-a-kind romance sure to make you jealous (and excited).

NSFW. Contains spanking, erotic humiliation, ageplay, ABDL, exhibitionism, lezdom, and consensual non-con. For readers 18+ only. All characters are 18+.

I'm Not a Little Girl (Really!) Vol. 3

Volume 3 in this series of romance novels continues the love story of Mary and Daphne right where Volume 2 left off, following 36-year-old Mary and 30-year-old Daphne, deeply in love and stuck in the cutest and kinkiest newlywed phase ever.

Once upon a time, our hero and narrator, Daphne, told her then-girlfriend Mary that she wanted their domestic discipline fetish to be their lifestyle. Fast forward to married life, and Daphne finds herself subject to strict and loving discipline from her doting wife that even Daphne's best bambi eyes can't get her out of.

Mary continues to lean into ageplay and "special undies" for Daphne as she insists she's not a little, gets herself into plenty of trouble, and ends up needing the padding for her sore bottom. Daphne does her best to be Mary's good girl, and it gets harder as quarantine continues and she struggles to keep herself entertained in ways that don't end with her over Mary's knee.

Daphne is madly in love with her wife and wants nothing so much as her approval, and of course Mary loves her Daphne and wants nothing so much as to see her safe and happy. These two sweethearts are sure to titillate you and make you jealous of their lovey-dovey relationship.

Theirs is a one-of-a-kind romance sure to make you jealous (and excited).

NSFW. Contains spanking, erotic humiliation, ageplay, ABDL, exhibitionism, lezdom, and consensual non-con. For readers 18+ only. All characters are 18+.

I'm Not a Little Girl (Really!) Vol. 4

Volume 4 in this series of romance novels continues the love story of Mary and Daphne right where Volume 3 left off, following 36-year-old Mary and 30-year-old Daphne, deeply in love and stuck in the cutest and kinkiest newlywed phase ever.

Once upon a time, our hero and narrator, Daphne, told her then-girlfriend Mary that she wanted their domestic discipline fetish to be their lifestyle. Fast forward to married life, and Daphne finds herself subject to strict and loving discipline from her doting wife that even Daphne's best bambi eyes can't get her out of.

Mary continues to nudge Daphne deeper into ageplay including a little trickery for her to experience what a squishy bottom feels like. For her part, Daphne gets herself into plenty of trouble and earns more than a few trips over Mary's knee. Daphne begins to think how she can slow her diapered downfall, trying to outwit her clever wife.

Daphne is madly in love with her wife and wants nothing so much as her approval, and of course Mary loves her Daphne and wants nothing so much as to see her safe and happy. These two sweethearts are sure to titillate you and make you jealous of their lovey-dovey relationship.

NSFW. Contains spanking, erotic humiliation, ageplay, ABDL, exhibitionism, lezdom, and consensual non-con. For readers 18+ only. All characters are 18+.

I'm Not a Little Girl (Really!) Vol. 5

Volume 5 in this series of romance novels continues the love story of Mary and Daphne right where Volume 4 left off, following 36-year-old Mary and 30-year-old Daphne, deeply in love and stuck in the cutest and kinkiest newlywed phase ever.

Once upon a time, our hero and narrator, Daphne, told her then-girlfriend Mary that she wanted their domestic discipline fetish to be their lifestyle. Fast forward to married life, and Daphne finds herself subject to strict and loving discipline from her doting wife that even Daphne's best bambi eyes can't get her out of.

Coping through the pandemic as Christmas approaches, Mary keeps her little Daffodil happy and well-disciplined why Daphne keeps Mary on her toes with her shenanigans. A major point of contention? The ageplay and absorbent undergarments Mary keeps nudging Daphne into, leaving her sputtering that she's not a little girl!

Daphne is madly in love with her wife and wants nothing so much as her approval, and of course Mary loves her Daphne and wants nothing so much as to see her safe and happy. These two sweethearts are sure to titillate you and make you jealous of their lovey-dovey relationship.

NSFW. Contains spanking, erotic humiliation, ageplay, ABDL, exhibitionism, lezdom, and consensual non-con. For readers 18+ only. All characters are 18+.

Done Adulting Volume 1

Eric decides his best chance at happiness is to leave the Earth, adopting himself out as a Little to the Diaper Dimension. But while he wants to leave, does he really want to give up his home and adulthood?

He takes a leap into the unknown, and he has a lot of adjustments to make as he learns what it means to be a Little and what it means to be loved.

This story, which takes place in the diaper dimension, is over 700 pages long. A great read of gentle ABDL themes and a classic hero's journey complete with a love story.

For readers 18+ only. All characters are 18+.

The Vacation: An ABDL Novel

John and Alice love each other deeply and share the closest of bonds: they both love diapers and ageplay. On this first vacation of their married life, Alice intends to use the week to help John work through some of his issues, including his fear of being padded in public. Will John resist or go along?

Alex's ABDL Anthology: Volume 1.

This volume of short stories are Alex's earliest published works, and while she's learned a lot an author, they're still a fun read for cute and kinky ABDL scenarios.

- In "Don't Color on the Wall", 27–year old Sara acts out to get attention, and her bottom gets more than she bargained for.

- In "After Dinner", she just can't hold it, even if she is almost 28.

- In "She's Just Not Ready Yet," it's time to reconsider potty training for a 27–year–old woman.

- In "An Audience," it's not the first time Sara has come over to Abby's house and found her husband doing corner time.

- And in "Unexpected Visitors," Ben is learning what it means to not be ashamed of his incontinence, even in front of his new neighbors.

For readers 18+ only. All characters are 18+.

Printed in Great Britain
by Amazon

59774669R00117